AFTER THE SNAP

LA WOLVES DEFENSE
BOOK 2

CADENCE KEYS

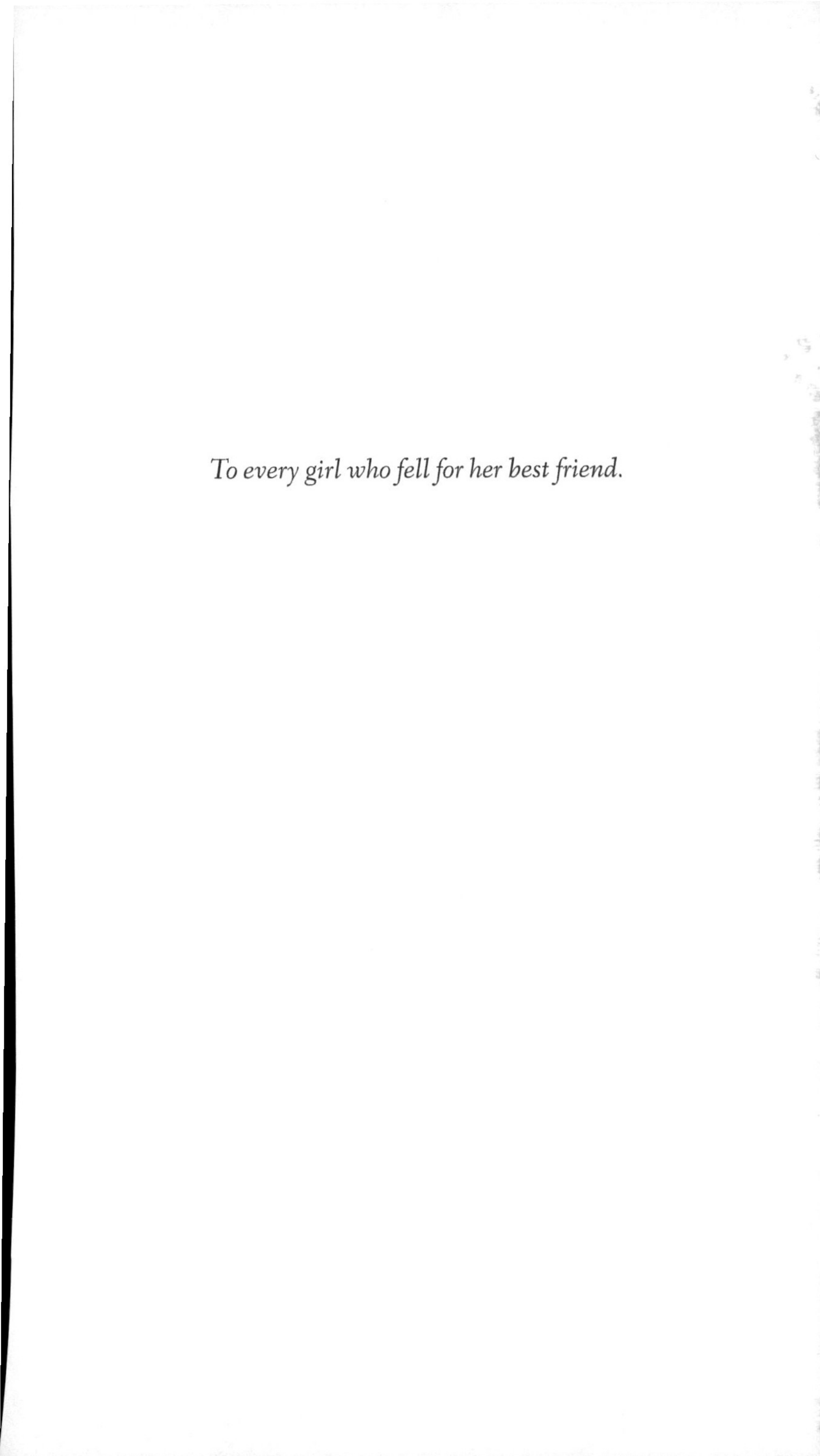

To every girl who fell for her best friend.

PLAYLIST

"Crave"—Paramore
"You Belong With Me"—Taylor Swift
"Blindsided"—Kelsea Ballerini
"Assembly Required"—Olivia Penalva
"Foolish One (Taylor's Version)"—Taylor Swift
"See, I'm Sorry"—Seafret
"I Live In Patterns"—Taylor Janzen, Alix Page
"Golden Age"—Rosie Darling
"Tension"—JP Saxe
"I Don't Want to Lose You"—Luca Fogale
"j's lullaby (darlin' i'd wait for you)"—Delaney Bailey
"Those Eyes"—New West
"No Right To Love You"—Rhys Lewis
"Yours"—Evann McIntosh
"Save Me"—Noah Kahan

Listen now on Spotify!

Dominic

PROLOGUE

It's too quiet. For days now, an eerie silence has settled in my house as hospice arrived to do what they could to ease my mom's pain as she slipped away from me second by second. I knew this day was coming from the first time my parents sat me down and broke the news that she'd been diagnosed with terminal cancer. But knowing something's coming doesn't necessarily make it any easier to handle.

The shrill clang of the doorbell breaks the silence, and I rush to the door before she can press it again. There's only one person I've invited over since my mom's diagnosis. Only one person who I trust to be here, to see the only vulnerability I have.

When I open the door, Alayna—or Laney as I've started calling her since no one else does and I wanted a nickname that was just mine—stands there with a bundle of fresh flowers and her backpack strapped to her back. We were paired together on a project last year in junior English and instantly clicked. Despite coming from two different crowds, I kept talking to her after that project, and now that we're nearing the end of our senior year, I can say without a doubt she's my best friend.

"Hey, I thought your mom might like some fresh flowers to brighten up her room, and these sunflowers looked so happy," she says, her deep-blue eyes shining with kindness. Her honey-blonde hair sways around her shoulders in the light breeze.

It takes me a second to realize the stretch of my lips is a small smile—probably the first one I've had since the last time Laney and I hung out. She's the only one who can get me to smile anymore. I'm afraid of the day when not even she will be able to get that reaction from me.

Dread pools in my stomach because I know that day is getting close and I'm nowhere near ready. Is anyone ever ready to lose a parent? Especially the one who has always understood them?

"She'll love them," I say, my voice rough. I step aside and let Laney in.

"How's she doing today?" she asks in a soft voice. Can she pick up on how my whole house has turned into a tomb as we wait for cancer to finally steal my mom from us?

I clear my throat again, the words scraping out. "Not well. Every day she gets a little worse."

Her soft hand slides into mine and squeezes, offering me comfort she knows words can't provide. We walk silently up the stairs toward my mom's room, my hand still holding hers tight. Each step closer always makes my stomach clench because I never know what I'm going to find.

But when I turn the corner to the hallway that leads to my mom's room, I halt in my tracks and my stomach twists sharply.

What the fuck?

I pull my hand from Laney's and curl it into a fist, hatred ripping through me until I swear literal smoke is coming out of my ears.

In front of the closed door leading to my mom's room stands my dad and her nurse—kissing.

They pull apart, staring at each other for a moment, something passing between them I'm too young or too pissed off to understand.

"You're a fucking piece of shit." The words rip from my throat, my limbs feeling hot and heavy with the anger pulsing through me, and a sickening feeling coiling in my stomach until I wonder if I'll actually vomit.

My dad's eyes widen, and that asshole has the nerve to take a step closer to me. "Dom. I can explain."

"Fuck you." I glare at the nurse. "And fuck you too."

"Dominic," my dad's voice is like a whip lashing across the room. "That's enough. Give me a minute to—"

"To what? To come up with some bullshit excuse for why you're cheating on Mom with her *fucking nurse*. You both can go to hell."

I'm not about to stick around to see what lame excuse he's planning to come up with. Instead, I turn around and go to my room. I can sense Laney close on my heels, but she doesn't try to talk to me or cool me down. Once again, she always seems to know what I need when I need it, and right now I don't need anyone to talk to me until I've cooled the fuck down.

I slam my door behind her when we get into my room and then I pace back and forth in front of my window that overlooks our large backyard. My parents bought this house because of the property. They wanted me to have a place to run around and be a kid. It's one of the nicest houses in our small town in northern Idaho, but right now I can't see anything but red. All the memories of a happy childhood with two parents who were so obviously in love with each other are now incinerated by the vision of my dad kissing another woman—while my mom lies dying in the next room.

"I can't believe he fucking did this to her. They were college sweethearts, and he goes and disrespects her with her own fucking nurse while she's dying?!"

I spin around and Laney is staring, her lips parted like she wants to say something, but no words come out. I start pacing again, clenching and releasing my fists that ache with the urge to punch something. But buried under all the anger boiling inside me is a deep hurt.

My parents were endgame. They were the couple all my friends always looked up to. They used to make out in the kitchen until I would gag and tell them to get a room. It grossed me out, but I never doubted that their love was real. It's the kind of love I aspired to have when I grew up.

Now, it's tainted.

Did he ever really love her? Has he cheated before? Why now? He couldn't wait until she was gone, but instead had to do it right outside her room? He probably wouldn't even have to wait that long.

My gut twists until I feel nauseous. My nose stings and my throat tightens as my vision blurs. I reach out to brace myself against the wall as the first tear falls. I suck in a sharp breath when I feel Laney's soft touch on my back, but it's that simple tender gesture that breaks the dam.

I fall to my knees and bury my head in my hands, releasing everything I've been holding in. I can't lose my mom. She can't leave me, not with *him*. Not after what I just witnessed.

What am I supposed to do without her?

A choked sob escapes and I try to stifle the noise, even if I know there's no use fighting the tears. I've been holding them back too long. All the while, Laney rubs gentle circles on my back, her presence a balm to my bottomless pain.

I reach back and grab her hand, holding it tight, acknowledging what she's doing even if I don't have the words right now to thank her. I can't lose her either. I squeeze her hand tighter as fear coils in my stomach. I need Laney. She can't leave me too. She squeezes my hand back as if she can read my thoughts, and some relief works its way through the fear.

There's a knock on my door, but neither of us acknowledge it. Then the click of the latch as the door swings open. I sit up and spin around to tell my dad to get the fuck out, but the devastation on his face halts any words on my tongue. My heart sinks to my stomach and I'm shaking my head in denial before his choked words even reach me, because I already know what he's going to say, and my whole world shifts under my feet.

"She's gone."

ONE

Alayna

Each headline is worse than the last, and yet I read every single one, a glutton for punishment. I should be used to this feeling by now. He's been pulling this shit for months, but for some reason it's *this* betrayal, this complete letdown that obliterates me as each word I read about Dom's latest scandal buries itself inside me. He seriously bailed on me at his own fucking birthday party for *her*.

Jen Summers.

Sure, she's gorgeous. All petite, with flawless skin and perky, fake boobs—only the best for an heiress turned Hollywood starlet. I bet she's a spinner. Bile rises in my throat as I imagine the many positions they could've been in when her husband found them in bed together.

What the fuck was Dom thinking? He's done a lot of stupid shit—more and more lately, which has been concerning—but never would I have expected this from him. He *hates* infidelity. Especially after what his dad did to his mom. Something about the story doesn't quite fit, but I'm too hurt to dive too deep into it.

I've been secretly—stupidly—in love with my best

friend, Dominic Smith, for as long as I can remember. When we were first paired together for a group project in high school, I thought it was going to be torture because we couldn't be more different. I was the quiet math nerd who was in math club and knowledge bowl, and Dom was this enigmatic powerhouse who got flirty smiles from the girls and high fives from the guys whenever he walked down the hall. But Dom surprised me. Instead of being the stereotypical jock I'd pinned him as, he was down-to-earth, fun, and carefree, but also completely and utterly dedicated to football. His passion for the game was contagious, and it wasn't long before he'd taught me about the different positions, plays, and terminology in between our project work.

Somewhere along the line, I found myself antsy with anticipation for every day that I knew we'd be working together. When the new unit rolled around and our teacher switched up the groups, I was devastated, not only because I was paired with Tim Ruggerts who had a nasty habit of eating hot Cheetos right before class and getting the cheese left over on his fingers everywhere, but also because I was going to miss my time with Dom. We didn't hang out outside of class, and I'd never felt such an instant connection with anyone as I did with him.

One night not long after the new groups were assigned, I was drowning my sorrows in a pint of Ben and Jerry's when my phone beeped with a text message. Imagine my surprise when the unknown number belonged to Dom. He'd asked a friend of mine for my number because he was completely lost on the unit assignments, and his new partner was obsessed with herself.

Thus began our friendship—and my completely one-sided crush. Dom became my lifeline through the struggles of senior year and the crippling fear that I wouldn't get the scholarship I needed in order to attend my dream school, Boise State. My dad had gone there, and I spent my whole life dreaming of the day I'd get to call myself a Bronco too. When my acceptance came in with a scholarship that covered all of my tuition, Dom was the first person I ran to. And when he announced his acceptance and football scholarship to Boise State, I was the first one he told—before it became headline news of our small Idaho town.

I thought college might be a fresh start for us, a chance to maybe take our friendship to the next level. I couldn't have been more wrong. I became Dom's go-to girl for everything but the one thing I wanted—okay, maybe two things.

His heart and his penis.

But the death of his mom—coupled with his dad's infidelity and then subsequent marriage—fucked with his head in a way I never saw coming. Dom became your stereotypical college football guy. He dated vapid cheerleaders and girls who were most likely to become models or social media famous. It was impressive if they could even carry a conversation that wasn't focused on celebrity gossip or the latest social media trend—if they even bothered to look up from their phone at all. Sometimes it seemed like he dated every girl but me.

There were days I wanted to hate him but I couldn't. As much as he was a player both on and off the field, he was also ultimately down to his core—deep, *deep* down lately—a good guy, and at the end of every day I was the person he reached out to. I was the friendship he maintained even at times when I would try to pull away to soothe my bruised heart. But he'd always pull me back asking if I was okay, seeking information for what was bothering me and how he could fix it.

But he couldn't fix what he didn't feel, and I didn't want

to see a look of pity on his face when I confessed what had become my deepest secret. I wasn't going to be desperate enough to throw myself at him when it was clear how he felt. I'd promised myself I would never be a man's second choice. I'd seen my mom put herself in that position too many times after my dad died when I was eight.

I can admit now that I've been waiting for him to see me —not just as his best friend, but as a woman—which is laughable as I sit here watching the entertainment media outlets go on and on about Dom's latest scandal. Shame and self-loathing swirl uncontrollably in my gut, and I feel like the most pathetic doormat in existence. How did I get here? How did our friendship go from the one thing that felt solid in my life to the thing that makes me feel the lowest about myself?

Dom's been all I've seen for so long. I've imagined our future together more times than I care to admit. Those nights in college when we'd stay up until the early hours of the morning talking about nothing and everything. The nights we'd walk the track around the football field and talk about our dreams for the future. He always spoke of the future with me in it, and it gave me a stupid amount of hope that someday he'd realize what was right in front of him.

Now all I have to show for all the years I've loved him is a broken heart, wounded pride, and a sick twisty feeling in my stomach.

I don't think I can do this anymore.

I can't keep being the one he's always coming back to when I don't actually mean what I want to mean to him. I can't keep being the one who always picks up the pieces for him. The woman who's always his shoulder, his support, despite the fact that he takes it for granted. Time and time again.

Images flash on the screen of other women Dom's been spotted with in the past few months as they continue to discuss his series of recent scandals and love life. Gorgeous women with figure-hugging dresses—showing off their tight abs, trim waists, toned legs, and thigh gaps. I've never had a thigh gap a day in my life. My breasts aren't as big as I wish they were for my size fourteen frame. My stomach is more flab than ab, even if my weight is distributed fairly evenly, and my tall height of five feet nine helps. That pit in my stomach grows because the only times I've ever been self-conscious about my body are in moments like this when I'm comparing myself to the models, actresses, and socialites Dom has gravitated toward since he joined the pros.

And all at once it hits me harder than it ever has. I'm never going to be enough for him. No matter what, I'm never going to be the kind of woman he wants. What's worse is that all of this pain is my own making. He's never promised me we'd be together in the future. He never tried to kiss me, not even when he was drunk. This has all been on me.

I can't keep waiting for him to *see* me. To want me. To love me the way I've always loved him. I toss back a gulp of my wine and swallow down the bitterness and hurt threatening to bring me even more pain. No. No more. I deserve more—better.

The point of the matter is that I've let Dom treat me like a doormat one too many times, and now the truth is hitting me like a football to the face.

It's time to move on.

TWO

Dominic

After the snap, it's always chaos on the field—coordinated chaos, but chaos, nonetheless. Bodies are moving everywhere, the ball is getting ready to launch into the air, but you have no idea where its target is. My job as cornerback is to see the bigger picture of all this chaos, to focus on where the ball is going to go and get there to end the play before the team can make too much forward progress.

If only things were that simple in my own life.

Unfortunately, the chaos I'm currently sitting through seems to have no end in sight, and I'm at a complete loss for how to stop this chaos from running roughshod right over me. I've fucked up a lot—more in the last few months than ever before—but this time seems to have stirred up a shit-storm not even I could have prepared for.

Come on, Laney. Pick up the damn phone.

I grip my phone hard and close my eyes when it goes to voicemail. Again.

Fuck.

"Dom? You ready?" My agent, Trey, pokes his head out of the nearest door, and I reluctantly nod. I'd feel more ready for this meeting if my best friend would answer her fucking phone.

I feel like I'm going into fucking battle here, and I really need to talk to Alayna. She's never failed to center me, even when the ground was crumbling beneath my feet. And right now the ground is exceptionally shaky. My career is on the line, and some days it feels like that's the only thing I have besides Laney.

My phone vibrates in my hand and I jerk it up, glancing at the screen like a teen girl waiting for her crush to call, only to roll my eyes when I see the caller. Since it's not Laney, I decline the call and tuck my phone in my pocket. Whatever my dad has to say to me can wait until I'm in a better frame of mind to deal with his bullshit.

The atmosphere when I walk into the room is tense, which does nothing to ease the tightness in my chest, but Trey still tries to give me a reassuring smile. He's been with me since the beginning and weathered every storm, but the edges of his smile are brittle like even he knows this was the final straw and we're dealing with something unprecedented for me.

It wasn't even that this was the worst thing I've ever done. It was just the straw that broke the camel's back. It was one thing too many, and even I can admit I fucked up.

I've *been* fucking up, but a part of me didn't care. I've been invincible for so long. You can get away with a lot when you're attractive and making millions of dollars a year. It didn't matter that my coaches were up my ass about my increasingly reckless behavior. It didn't matter when my best friends Gabe, Ty, and Romel called me out for being an inconsiderate ass.

None of it mattered until Alayna's silence. Every call in the past week has gone unanswered. Every text left on read.

I'm not sure why it's her actions that tipped me over into realizing how badly I've fucked things up. Maybe because she's seen me at my lowest and still never left my side. Or because she knows everything about me, more than even the guys, and still stuck around. Maybe because at the end of the day, she's always been my rock, my strength, whether she knows it or not.

And now I'm feeling lost without her.

I slide my hand into my pocket over my phone, hoping it'll vibrate with a text or call from her, but it doesn't.

"Dom, I'd like to introduce you to Shawna Cramer. She's from the new PR firm and has dealt with some very big public scandals."

Shawna stands and extends her hand. Her pantsuit is tailored to fit her trim frame perfectly, her brown hair straight and smooth down her back. She may look small compared to me, but her handshake is firm, and she holds my gaze with the confidence of the toughest linebacker who knows he can pummel anyone he comes across.

"Wish we didn't have to meet like this," I say with a slight raise of my lips in what might pass as a tight smile, my usual carefree grin nowhere to be found.

"I'm used to meeting people at their worst," she says with joking smirk. "Don't worry about a thing, Dom. We'll get this all cleared up in no time." She gestures to a man sitting next to her. "This is my assistant, Spencer. He'll be taking notes."

I extend my hand, and he shakes it quickly before resuming his position at Shawna's side and picking up his pen. They both seem competent, and I trust Trey's judgment, but that tightness is still there and when I sit, I can't stop my knee from bouncing under the table.

"So, what's the plan?" I ask. This isn't my first rodeo with a PR company or needing to clean up a mess.

"We've already written up a statement," she says as she slides a piece of paper from an organized pile next to her across the table toward me. "With your approval, we'll send it to the media outlets."

My lips pull down and my brows furrow as I read the statement. "This puts all the blame on Jen." Jen Summers, the woman I met at my birthday bash who told me she was separated from her husband and looking for a rebound. I was drunk—not that that's a good excuse, but it was certainly a factor—and she was hot. I didn't think much of it past that until we were alone in her house and a man burst into the room in a rage. Turns out she wasn't separated at all. I was the other man, something I promised myself a long time ago I'd never be after discovering my own father's affair.

Adultery is a hard pass for me, so not only is this scandal an embarrassment and the final straw for my coaches, but it's also made my self-loathing soar to an all-time high.

I need to get my shit together.

Shawna nods once. "Correct. You were innocent. You thought you were hooking up with an available woman. It's appropriate that the blame should land on her, and it's easy to paint women in a bad light in the media. No one will question it."

"Absolutely not," I say, my voice hard and firm.

Everyone goes still for a second before Trey leans over to whisper in my ear. "Shawna is the best—"

Without looking away from Shawna, I say in a clear voice for all to hear, "If she's the best, then she can figure out another angle. I'm not playing the blame game here. Was I lied to? Yes. But I'm fully responsible for my own actions. She's famous enough I could've—and should've—questioned it, but I didn't. I was irresponsible and made a poor judgment. That's on me. Not on her. I won't add to her issues, for the very reason that women too often get the blame for things that aren't their fault, or at least not entirely. It takes two."

She narrows her eyes slightly, but then sits taller. "Fine. We'll go a different route. If you insist on owning up to it, then we can do that. You might get some begrudging respect for taking that approach." She nods and her eyes light up like she's liking that idea more and more. She turns to her assistant and gives him a list of tasks to do and a new statement that they'll need to write up.

We discuss a timeline for giving my statement and setting up a press conference. After we have a pretty solid game plan, she turns back to her notes and then back to me with a fire in her eyes that makes whatever relief I had slowly drain away.

"We need to change your public image."

"Isn't that what the statement's for?" I ask.

"That's a start for this specific incident, but you've had quite a few scandals over the last year. Trey says there's concern you might get traded because the Wolves don't want the embarrassment you bring to the team, no matter how good you are on the field."

My stomach clenches and I snap my gaze to Trey. He winces and then nods, confirming my worst fears. There'd been rumblings, and Coach Denton and Coach Fairbright have talked to me more than once, but I guess I thought as long as I kept playing well, there was no way they'd trade me. I'm one of the core members of the Fierce Four—the four key players in our defensive line that have become famous in the league for our skills. We're crushing it this year, and there's a good chance we'll make it to the Super Bowl if we keep it up. Would they still trade me if I'm a critical component of that success?

The look on Trey's face says it's possible, and that does nothing to ease my doubts.

"I've got some ideas I'd like to run by you on how we can change your image. If we start right away with some of the changes and ease into my big idea then everyone will assume this scandal was the catalyst for your change. We can spin it all in our favor and get you from wild party boy to something more wholesome and lovable."

Shawna's too excited about this idea, which makes me skeptical that I'm going to like anything about it, but if it'll save my career and my spot on the Wolves, I have to try.

"Okay, what've you got?"

"For starters, no more wild parties. That's going to be the quickest way to clean up your image. Maybe join some of your teammates at their next charitable function. We don't want to go too far into the charitable acts yet because that'll look fake from a mile away. But if it looks like you're there to support your friends and then you start getting into your own charity events, it'll be seamless."

"Alright. I don't have a problem with any of that." I can admit the partying was getting out of control, and it's probably a good idea to lie low and take a break for a while.

"Is that it?"

"Not quite," she says. "You need an image overhaul when it comes to your relationships with women, so I propose that you commit to a semi-long-term relationship. I've got a list of potential women who would also benefit from the match, and NDAs are ready for any of them. I've had our lawyers write up a contract laying out all the expectations—public dates, some mild PDA, social media posts, things like that—and what each candidate would get out of the relationship-"

"Wait a second," I interrupt her. "You want me to get into a *fake* relationship?"

She smiles like I've said something funny. "Well, I don't expect you to have a woman already, not with the way you go through women as it is. So, I've preselected some options—"

"No." I cut her off again. Not because I hate the idea of a relationship, but because I refuse to put on a show with someone I don't know. Someone I don't trust.

"I have someone."

The words are out of my mouth before my brain even has a chance to catch up, but I don't take them back and I sure as fuck don't regret them. Because I do have someone. Someone I trust with my life, my secrets, my career. The only someone I'd ever do something this insane with.

Shawna's eyebrows practically shoot up to her hairline. "You do?"

"Yeah," I say, more confident with each second that the idea settles.

"And she'll go along with this?"

Now, that's the question. "She will," I say, even as uncertainty slithers inside me.

She has to. There's no way I can do this without her.

THREE

Alayna

My phone rings for the hundredth time, and I let out a frustrated groan before silencing it, throwing it in my desk drawer and then slamming it closed. My coworker Tessa walks into my office right as it vibrates again, and I scowl at the closed desk drawer.

"Boy problems?"

I point my scowl at her instead. "Why would you say that?"

She points at my face. "Because I know that look. I used to see it in the mirror all the time before Mike and I got married. It shouts boy trouble." She takes a seat in one of the two chairs on the other side of my desk. "I didn't realize you were seeing anyone."

"I'm not."

She smiles and picks at a nonexistent piece of lint on her immaculately ironed pants. "Ah, so it's Dom then?"

I let out a sigh and sag back against my chair. I don't usually talk to people about Dom, but Tessa and I worked our way up from the bottom of this company together. She's one of the few people I've opened up to outside of the LA

Wolves found family I have via Dom. And she's the only one I trust not to go blabbing to the media about anything I share—I tested her many times.

"I think our friendship is over."

As soon as the last word leaves my mouth, my phone rattles around in my drawer and she arches a brow. "Does he know that?"

"Not yet."

"So you're just ignoring his calls, hoping he'll take the hint?"

"No. I'm going to tell him. I'm just mad and don't have the words right now."

"And what words are you looking for exactly?"

I stare at her and nibble the inside of my lip.

"You planning to tell him you're in love with him finally?"

My jaw drops open and she rolls her eyes dramatically. "Oh please. I figured it out years ago. You're ridiculously protective of Mr. Jesse Williams lookalike."

"I can be protective and not have feelings for him."

"You could, but you *do* have feelings for him."

A new worry infiltrates. "Is it that obvious?" Has he been able to tell all this time and I've just looked pitiful to him? Mortification heats my cheeks at the thought that he's known about my true feelings this whole time.

Her gaze softens and she leans forward. "Alayna, relax. No, it's not that obvious. I'm just exceptionally good at reading people, and you've actually let me in. I doubt anyone else would realize, especially not Dom. Let's face it, men aren't always the most perceptive beings, and Dom is no exception. But...I mean, would it be so bad if he did know?"

I've asked myself that question a million times over the

years. There have been countless times when I've opened my mouth to tell him—especially those late nights when it was just the two of us and our conversations would become unexpectedly deep. Many a time I would look at him and the words would be *right there* on the tip of my tongue, begging to be released. Wondering what would happen if I spoke them. Would he reciprocate those feelings? Would he take the leap with me?

Would he love me?

But the moment always passed before the words were set free, so I'd swallow them down. And then I'd spend the next several weeks or months being his gal pal while I watched him flirt with every sorority girl on campus, or the cheerleaders on the sidelines, or the girls who would grind on him at dance parties.

Over time, it got a lot easier to keep those words to myself. Probably because it became more and more obvious that Dom couldn't possibly reciprocate them.

"It would change our entire relationship, so yes, it would be that bad," I say, answering Tessa's question.

"It sounds like you're planning to change the relationship anyway, so what could it hurt? What if it changed it for the better? What if he's as afraid as you are?"

"Dom's not afraid of anything, except maybe losing football." Nothing is more important to him than football. I'm a close second, and I've always relished that position in his life, even if I wished I was the most important like he's always been to me.

I completely drop my guard now because it's exhausting leaving it up for everyone, and I trust Tessa.

"I feel like such an idiot, Tess," my voice cracks.

Sympathy coats her strong Italian features, and she reaches out a hand to rest it over mine. "You're not an idiot."

I scoff. "I am. I've wasted *years*. For what? I've spent nearly the last decade loving a man who has only ever seen me as a friend. Don't say that's not pathetic because it feels pathetic."

"We can't pick and choose who we love." She tilts her head to the side. "Is all this coming up because of the Jen Summers thing?"

I shake my head, then tilt it back until it rests against the high back of my chair. My gaze locks on the white ceiling as if it'll give me some answers. "I helped him plan that whole stupid birthday party and he ditched me for her."

"He's been doing that a lot more lately, it seems."

I nod. He has. And I'm probably the only person in the world who knows what started his spiral. I can't blame him for reacting poorly. His relationship with his dad has been complicated since we were in high school and he discovered his dad was having an affair with the in-home nurse he'd hired to take care of Dom's mom who was dying from cancer—the same nurse he married about a year after Dom's mom passed away. Regardless of their history, I know he's not taking the news about his dad's pancreatic cancer well.

But that's not my secret to tell.

And that doesn't give him carte blanche to treat me like garbage. Not after all the years we've been friends. Not after all the highs and lows we've been through together.

"You know why he's spiraling, don't you?" she asks.

"It doesn't matter. It doesn't excuse anything."

My phone vibrates again, and both of us just stare at each other as it rumbles against the inside of my drawer.

"You're really not going to answer that?" she asks.

"Not yet." I will...when I actually know what to say and how to say it. You can't just end a decade-long friendship over the phone, but I'm also not sure I'm strong enough to say what needs to be said to his face.

Tessa leans forward, her brow furrowed with concern. "Are you sure this is what you want?"

I let out a sigh. "I think it's what I need. I can't wait for him anymore."

She gets a look on her face like there's more she wants to say, but then shakes her head slightly and smiles. "Does that mean I can finally set you up with Mike's brother? He saw a picture of you once and still asks about you."

I arch my brow. "Really? You waited all of two seconds before suggesting a blind date?"

She sits back in her chair, a cheeky smile on her face. "It's not really a blind date. You've both seen pictures of the other, and it could be good for you to go on a date where you're actually ready to give the guy a chance."

I nibble my lip, unsure, until my phone buzzes again in my drawer. God, how many times is he going to call me before he quits and waits until I'm ready to come to him?

Thinking about him and why I'm mad this time only brings to mind the images of him and Jen Summers that have lived rent free in my head since the news broke. That's the push I need to square my shoulders with firm resolution.

"Let's do it."

Tessa's eyebrows shoot up. "For real?"

"Yep," I say, my voice strong and sure, even as my heart beats frantically in my chest and my stomach twists with nerves. I haven't been on a date in over a year, and that was a disaster. In fact, most of my dates have been duds, and the few relationships I've had—if you can even call them that— barely lasted a month or two before they ended. Sometimes it was because of me calling it off, and sometimes it was because they couldn't handle Dom's position in my life.

Either way, they ended and I was never all that heartbroken about it.

But if I'm going to really move on, that means putting myself out there. It's clear that Dom will never see me as anything more than a friend, so it's time to let go of the idea of *us* once and for all.

FOUR

Dominic

The elevator dings as I arrive on Laney's floor, and my steps pound the otherwise quiet hall leading toward her apartment. My back teeth grind in frustration because she's still not answering my calls or texts, which isn't like her. She's frozen me out before, but never like this. The silent treatment isn't her style, which is why it bothers me so much that she's pulling this shit now.

We've always been straight with each other, so why won't she just yell at me and we can move on?

I knock on her door with one hand while her favorite coffee—the one she only lets herself have on special occasions—is in a to-go cup in my other. She opens the door and leans against it while her shoulders sag and she lets out a heavy breath. I can't tell if it's exasperation with me or resignation, but something about the latter bothers me more.

"You couldn't wait for me to call you back when I was ready?"

I love that she cuts right to the chase. It's one of my favorite traits of hers. "It couldn't wait. I need to talk to you."

Her eyes search mine, and there's something in them that makes my gut clench. It's not a look she's ever given me before, and I thought I knew all her looks. Before I can analyze it too much, she sighs again and steps back, opening the door wider so I can step inside.

Her apartment is bright and airy with large windows that let in natural light and give a decent view. She's got splashes of color around the room that make it feel vibrant without it being too eclectic. A large white shag carpet is spread out in front of her couch, and I automatically slip out of my shoes so I don't get it dirty. It also feels plush underneath my feet, and there's something incredibly relaxing about it. I take a seat on the couch and lean back, my chest expanding with the first real breath I've taken all day.

Fuck, it feels good to be in her space. It's always soothing to be here, and I wish I could figure out what exactly she does to make her place feel so calming so I could replicate it at my house.

"So, what was so important it couldn't wait a few days?"

I turn my head to take her in. She's standing with her arms crossed, leaning her back against the edge of her kitchen island.

"Come sit down and I'll tell you."

"I'd rather not."

We stare at each other, and something new arches between us—I don't know if I like it. "Are you really that pissed at me?"

She looks down at the floor, breaking eye contact, and my chest tightens, my gaze locked on her with an almost desperate desire for her to look at me again.

"Laney."

She shakes her head and looks back up, but her expression is guarded. "Dom...I don't...We...Our priorities are too different these days, and I think we've grown too far apart for our friendship to continue."

For how choppy she started, the tail end of her sentence escapes her mouth like a priest just exorcised a demon from her. She stares at me, her eyes a little wide, but I doubt they're as wide as mine.

"You..." I have to clear my throat while my brain scrambles to make sense of what she just said. "You think we shouldn't be friends anymore?" Something akin to panic surges wildly inside my chest. "No," I say, standing up because I can't sit with all this energy suddenly pulsing through my body.

Her lips tilt down in a frown. "What the hell do you mean 'no'?"

I shake my head, then scrub a hand over my short, black hair. "No. We've been friends too long for you to just throw me away like I don't mean anything."

"Dom—"

"No," I say again, knowing I sound like a broken record, but I have to stop this, no matter what. I can't lose her. "Yell at me, tell me how disappointed you are in me, anything but ending the most important relationship in my life."

"Is that even true anymore?"

I stop my frantic pacing and stare at her, my heart thundering in my chest as pain ricochets around my ribs. Have I really fucked up that badly that she questions what she means to me? The bad publicity, the risk of losing my spot on the Wolves, none of it hits me as hard as that one question coming out of her mouth.

I clench my jaw and fight the urge to walk up to her and pull her into my arms to hold her tight like I desperately need to. But the look in her eyes and stiffness of her body tell me that kind of physical touch wouldn't be accepted right now. So, I dig deep and try to find the words that can offer some kind of reparation for the damage I've caused.

The doubt my actions have planted in her mind.

"Laney, you're the single most important person in my life." I take a step closer because I can't stop myself. "I love you—"

She flinches as if I've just struck her, and my gut clenches. We've said "I love you" or "love you" before, but she's never had such a visceral negative reaction, and it makes any other words I'd prepared halt.

I'm missing something.

"Laney?"

"I can't do this with you right now, Dom. I need some space, okay? Can you respect that?"

I'm only a few feet away from her, but it feels like we're miles apart, and that sick feeling in my stomach grows.

"Don't you have a game today?" she asks, and when I nod, she says, "You should probably go then, so you're not late. I'm sure the coaches are watching your every move right now."

They are, but for the first time in as long as I can remember, football doesn't feel like the priority.

She is.

But I can tell she means it when she says she wants space, and I'm not about to force myself on her. I know her well enough to know if her mind's set on space, she won't hear anything I have to say. My only fear is leaving her with her thoughts because for the first time, I'm not certain I can fix this. She's never said she thought we shouldn't be friends before.

"We're not done," I say, my voice stronger than I feel. "I'll call you after my game, okay?"

She looks at me, her eyes drooping at the edges and

holding a sadness I haven't seen before. "Not tonight. Space, remember?"

I grind my molars together again and then mumble, "Fine."

She offers me a weak smile, then opens the door, and with reluctant steps, I leave.

I shove my fingers over my hair and then lean my elbows on my knees, my hands dangling between my legs as I try to get my head together. This is a critical game—it determines whether we're going to the NFC Championship or not—and I can't do a fucking thing right. Tyler Russell, a free safety and one of the core members of the Fierce Four, eyes me and gives me a sympathetic smile. He's the only one I've told about Laney so far, even though I know I'll tell Gabe and Romel eventually. Gabe Romero and Romel Watson make up the other half of the Fierce Four. These guys are my brothers in all the ways that matter. They've had my back since we all joined the team, and there's a reason we've become an unstoppable force in the league. I know I'm not carrying my weight the way I usually do, which only pisses me off more.

I've always been able to compartmentalize when it comes to football. Nothing else was ever more important.

Until now.

Romel comes and sits down next to me. "I know I'm fucking things up," I say.

"What's going on with you? Even after your other scandals, you were never this sloppy on the field. We need you out there, Dom. Wherever your head's at, I need you to get it back here." He points his finger to the ground between us.

"Do what you gotta do to get it straight." He leans closer and his voice lowers. "Our coaches need a reminder of why they can't let you go, not another reason for you to leave. You feel me?"

"I feel you." My voice is gruff. I don't say anything else, but I don't need to. These guys know me, almost as well as Laney. Romel knows I'll talk about it when I'm ready. Hell, I'm surprised Ty hasn't told him already.

He stands up and slaps me on the back before walking over where Gabe and Ty stand on the sidelines while I grab the tablet lying next to me and focus in on the plays I should know like the back of my hand. I can't mess this up anymore. It doesn't surprise me when a few minutes later, Gabe comes over and sits down. It seems like they're taking shifts checking in on me, and that solidifies my determination further. No matter what's going on in my personal life, I've got to pull it together for these guys.

"Are you okay?" he asks as he sits down.

"I'm sorry I've been playing like shit." I set the tablet down and rub my hand over my head, resting back along the bench, trying to look as composed as possible for the cameras watching the players on the sidelines. They can't see the waver in my voice, so the only thing tipping them off that I'm not up to my usual standards is my playing on the field. "I really fucked up this time," I add, not that I really needed to, but I've got to get some of this off my chest—like a release valve letting out some of the pressure that's built up.

"You can't be the first guy to get caught naked with a married celeb."

I grip my thigh on the side where the press won't notice in a lame attempt to help keep me composed. "She swore they were separated, but I couldn't care less about her." It's the truth, even if it pisses me off that her lie led me to this moment.

"You're talking about Alayna."

Hearing her name causes my composure to crack. "Yeah."

"You guys have been friends for a long time. She's dealt with your bullshit before. Maybe she just needs a little cooldown time."

I shake my head. "Not this time. She was pretty clear she was done." The words are like shards of glass ripping through me. I can still hear her words crystal clear as she said she thought our friendship was over. But it can't be over. It can't.

"She's going to be even more pissed if she finds out you played like a pussy because she got in your head. She might be cursing your name, but we both know she's a die-hard Wolves fan and wants to see us go to the Super Bowl."

Fuck, he's totally right. She'd be ripping me a new one if she was here to see me play like garbage. I turn my head to stare at Gabe. "So what you're saying is I need to pull my shit together?"

"Pretty much."

I huff out a laugh. His words are exactly what I needed to hear. "Are we straight?" I ask.

He slaps my back. "Yeah, man. We're good." He holds up a fist waiting for me to pound it, which I do. "Brothers forever," he says.

"Brothers forever."

Then he stands, rubs my hair, and pushes my head down.

"What the fuck, dude?"

"That's for telling Alayna about Taylor Swift," he says with a gleam in his eye even as he's fighting back a grin.

I fall back against the bench, my hand over my chest as a hearty laugh escapes for the first time in days. Shit. Laney must've told Gabe's new girlfriend about what huge secret Swifties we all are. Gabe smiles in victory before the play on the field ends and we're up.

I've got a job to do, and knowing Laney's probably watching—even if she's mad at me and convinced our friendship is over—drives me to play harder than I ever have.

Yes, I need to prove my worth to my coaches. But more importantly, I need to prove my worth to her. I need to show her I can keep my shit together.

She can't give up on me yet.

FIVE

Alayna

It would be a lot easier to let go of Dom if he wasn't leaning against the wall next to my front door when I get home from work—again.

I let out a resigned sigh. "I thought you agreed to give me space? Why can't you ever just let me ignore you until I'm ready?"

He pushes off the wall, and I hate the way my gut tightens with want. It's really unfair how attractive he is.

"Because I'm your best friend and we need to talk this out. I've let you have a few days, but now I need you to lay it all out for me so I know what it'll take to fix this. I miss you, Laney."

Now it's not just my gut clenching but my heart. God, this is fucking hard. I've loved this man for years, and hurting him feels a lot like hurting myself, but I know it's time. I can't keep going on like this.

Bile rises in my throat as a riot of nerves overwhelms me. This is it. He's left me no choice but to lay it all out right now.

"Fine, let's talk inside."

We walk into the room, and I move to my coat closet to put away my jacket and purse. As soon as the door clicks shut, he speaks.

"I can't lose you, Laney. I'll do whatever it takes to keep you in my life. That's a promise. And right now I need you more than ever." He rubs his black hair in a nervous gesture he's had for years. "My new PR team wants me to have a public relationship—a fake one—for the next six months to help repair my image. I don't want to do it unless I can pick the woman, and I want you."

The earnest expression on his face makes my stomach somersault—and not in a good way.

"You know me," he says. "We already spend a ton of time together. It won't feel awkward or forced to be seen in public on dates together. We can work on the fine details of what this all entails, but I need you, more than I ever have. You're the only woman I can do this with. And maybe we can even take that time to work through our own issues. I know you're mad at me about my birthday—"

"This isn't about your birthday."

His mouth snaps shut and his brows furrow. "It's not?"

"No, it's not."

"Then what's it about?"

I'm exhausted from this conversation and the hardest part hasn't even happened yet. "Dom..."

He steps closer, panic flaring in those light-blue eyes that have always held me hostage. "I'll give you whatever you want if you agree to do this with me, Laney. If you want space from me afterward, I'll give it to you, even if it fucking kills me."

I swallow thickly and then clear my throat. "Even if I

tell you I don't want to see or talk to you for a year...or longer?"

His jaw clenches and his nose flares, but then he nods. I know him well enough to know it's probably not that simple, and honestly, I don't think I can last six more months of this. I doubt he'll even want to do this fake relationship with me once I confess the secret I've kept from him for years.

"I don't think it's a good idea, Dom. I can't pretend to be your girlfriend," I say, swallowing down the building anxiety at finally confessing my feelings. My heart races and my breaths get short.

"Why not?" he asks, sounding genuinely confused now.

I close my eyes, because I can't bear to see the look of pity I know will appear in his gorgeous eyes when I spill my heart. "Because I love you."

"I love you too, but I don't see—"

"No. I'm *in love* with you."

Silence.

Utterly terrifying silence that leaves only the booming sound of my heart racing in my ears. I can't believe I just told him that. I can't believe I really did it, after all this time of holding back. Saying the words themselves was shockingly easy. It's the deafening silence that feels like a painful eternity in limbo, but I can't take back the words now that they're out there. I can't pretend I was joking. He'd know.

There's no going back.

More importantly, I don't want to.

I've kept my feelings to myself for too long. If I really want a new beginning, then it's time to be brutally and painfully honest.

After what feels like five minutes, but is likely only one,

I can't take the silence anymore, so I open my eyes. His crystal-blue gaze is locked on my face, but it isn't filled with the pity I expected. There's a deeper emotion there I can't name and that almost scares me more. He's not reacting the way I thought he would. He's not reacting at all. He seems frozen as he stares at me with his intense expression.

I stare at him for another minute, thinking he'll snap out of it and say something—anything—but he doesn't.

The minutes stretch longer and longer as we stare at each other until my heart is racing so fast, it's all I can hear.

"Dom?"

He blinks once, twice. Then, "I'm only asking for six months," he says, his voice deep and hoarse and his eyes not giving away anything.

I shake my head because he clearly doesn't get it. "You're asking for so much more than that. You're asking for me to pretend to date you when I have feelings for you. Feelings you don't reciprocate."

His Adam's apple bobs as he swallows. "You wouldn't be pretending."

My eyes bug out as I lean forward. "And you don't see why that might be hard for me?"

I thought his silence hurt, but this is so much worse.

The sting of tears burns my eyes and I know I'm only minutes away from losing it as my heart lies on the floor at his feet. Moving to the door, I open it and avoid his gaze. "You need to leave."

"Laney—"

"Get out, Dom." My voice is cold and devoid of emotion. I've had years of practice from all my interactions with my mom, but I never thought I'd have to do this with Dom.

He doesn't move for a moment, and then his heavy footfalls shuffle past me for the second time in less than a week. This time, I refuse to look up into those eyes that I've loved for so long. The second I shut the door with him on the other side, the tears fall, and I don't fight them.

I don't have any fight left.

SIX

Dominic

The TV screen in front of me is a blur as I zone out on my couch, my fingers wrapped around the neck of a beer bottle I haven't decided if I'm going to drink yet. I swore off alcohol after what happened with Jen, but Laney's confession has me questioning that decision.

No, not confession. Revelation.

I'm in love with you.

I never knew five words could have such an impact on me, but sure enough, I've been reeling since they left her lush, pink lips. I'm left with so many questions I'm not even sure where to begin. How long has she felt that way? And maybe most importantly, why the *fuck* didn't she say something sooner?

I cringe as I think about all the women she likely saw me flirting with over the last few years, especially this last year when I've admittedly been in a downward spiral. Was I hurting her that whole time?

My gut tightens painfully. The last thing I ever want to do is hurt Laney. I wasn't lying when I told her she's the most important relationship in my life. I feel lost without her.

The doorbell rings, pulling me out of my stupor. When I answer it, I'm not surprised to find Ty on the other side.

"Hey man, what's up?"

He comes in when I open the door wider in invitation. "I was in the neighborhood and thought I'd stop by to check in with you. See how things are going with Alayna."

He shrugs out of his jacket and sits on the couch. He's been here enough times to make himself comfortable.

"Want a beer?" I ask.

"Sure."

I grab him a beer and then take a seat on the other end of the couch, my now warm beer still held tightly in my hands. Ty takes a sip, watching me closely before settling back in the seat.

"So? What happened with Alayna?"

I lean forward to set the untouched beer on the coffee table. I'm not going to drink it, and there's no sense holding it any longer. Resting my elbows on my knees, I turn my head and admit what happened—because if there's anyone who can help me make sense of all this, it's Ty.

"She told me she loved me."

He smiles. "See, man, I told you there was nothing to worry about and she'd forgive you."

I'm already shaking my head. "No, she's *in love* with me."

His smile falls as his mouth parts in shock. "Wait, for real?"

I nod.

"Woah. I mean, the guys and I always wondered. She's hot. You'd have to be an idiot not to notice."

"Rub it in, why don't ya."

He leans forward, his pose mirroring mine. "Are you trying to tell me you never noticed how hot she is? You never thought about crossing the line from friends to more?"

Fuck, I really want that beer. Swallowing thickly, I admit, "Of course I noticed. And yeah, I thought about it back in high school."

Back before my life took a hard left turn and my mom died and my dad became someone I didn't know or trust. I couldn't rock the boat after that. Laney was the only solid thing in my life that kept me afloat. I wasn't going to sacrifice that just to get my rocks off.

"So what stopped you from pursuing her? I've never seen you hesitate when it comes to women."

Ty's been my wingman more times than I can count. He can pull in nearly as many girls as I do, although he usually doesn't. He doesn't talk about it, but I know he prefers something long-term. He's always been a guy who thrives in a relationship, but his last girlfriend was a real piece of work. I'd never seen a woman flip the switch from sane to crazy like Emily did. So while I was spiraling, he was trying to be a guy who can fuck without getting attached. I feel like a shit friend because here he is checking on me, and I realize I've never checked to see how he's been after Emily went crazy on him.

I lean back against the couch. "Fuck, dude. I've been a really shitty friend. I haven't asked you how things have been with you since Emily."

He arches a brow. "Talk about a change of subject. I'm fine. Now stop avoiding my questions."

I scowl at him which only makes him smile as he leans back on the couch and twists his body to face me.

"Seriously, what are you going to do about Alayna?"

"I don't know. I really don't."

"Do you think you could ever love her back?"

I look down at my hands. "I do love her, more than anyone else, but I don't know if I'm in love with her. I...I don't know what that kind of love feels like."

He smirks. "Well, in my experience, when you love someone, they're the one person you want to be around every day. The thought of losing them scares the shit out of you. You care more for them than anyone else—and ideally they feel the same way. And you think about them all the time. You want to make their life better and be the best version of yourself for them."

Well, fuck.

If it weren't for my spiral in the last year, all of those points would be true for Alayna. Before this fallout, we talked every day, even if it was just a few texts. But even with this tension between us, she's all I've thought about, even when my agent's been trying to get me to focus on football. Laney's been the priority. She's *always* been the priority, even if she doesn't believe that. But it's his last point that has my chest feeling tight. I've not been making her life better. I've made it worse with my actions because I couldn't see anything but my own pain and confusion over how to deal with what's happening with my dad.

"So?" he asks, pulling me out of my thoughts. "Do you feel any of that for Alayna?"

I swallow thickly and then have to clear my throat to push the words out. "Yeah," I croak. "Yeah, I do," I say again, a little stronger this time. "I didn't realize that's what it was."

Ty's eyes fill with sympathy. "Yeah, I hate to admit that women might be right, but sometimes we guys can be a little dense."

"Yeah," I say vacantly while my mind replays all my

past interactions with Laney with this new, very valuable information. But instead of making me feel excited and confident, dread fills my stomach. I've hurt her, repeatedly, because I was too stupid to see what was right in front of me.

"I don't know how to fix this," I confess.

"You should talk to her."

"She was pretty clear about wanting space."

"Maybe, but in my experience, space doesn't fix anything. It just delays the communication that's inevitable. You two will have to talk eventually to sort this out."

He's right, but I also know my words won't matter to her —not right now. An apology might, but if I tell her what I'm only now starting to realize about my feelings for her, she'll never believe me.

So I'll have to show her.

SEVEN

Alayna

I wasn't sure Dom would actually give me the space I'd asked for, but it's been three days since he showed up at my apartment for a second time, and I haven't heard a peep from him. I should be thankful that he's respecting my wishes, but I miss him.

Fiercely.

And I hate myself for it.

Is this some weird twist on Stockholm Syndrome? I don't know, but I do know that I'm nowhere near as invested in this blind date Tessa set up with her brother-in-law as I should be.

I choose a sexy little black dress that accentuates my curves and style my blonde hair in luscious beach waves. A smoky eye and red lipstick finish the look, but there's no excitement thrumming in my body like I hoped there would be. Instead, when the buzzer goes off announcing that Ben is here, I have to close my eyes and give myself a pep talk.

You're moving on. This is what moving on looks like, and you deserve to be taken out on a date and to have a good time. Tess wouldn't set you up with a dud.

I inhale deeply and then release it as I open my eyes, grab my purse, then head downstairs to meet him.

Ben is exactly like Tessa described him and how I remembered him from the one photo I saw. He's tall—at least six feet two—with a chiseled jawline covered in trim brown facial hair that isn't quite a beard, but doesn't make him look scruffy in the slightest. His warm, brown eyes light up when he sees me, and his mouth tilts up in an absolutely gorgeous smile. He's got the build of a football player, and I fight back a smile because Tess totally knows my type. This guy screams athlete, even if he's not one anymore.

"You're even more beautiful in person." His cheeks get pink. "Shit. I didn't mean to say that aloud, but Tessa held out on me. The picture I saw of you blew me away, but it still didn't do you justice."

I tuck my chin and fight back my own smile at his compliment. He delivers it so sincerely, but there's still no flutter or giddy excitement in my belly.

He opens the car door for me and I get in. On the way to the restaurant, he asks me how my day was and I tell him. There's definitely some first date awkwardness, but Ben is easygoing, and that awkwardness fades by the time we get to the restaurant.

As we order food and continue talking, I wait for a spark, anything, to ignite, but there's nothing.

Not a damn thing.

Ben is great. He checks off every box I could have for a good match. He's educated, has a stable job, and his own apartment. He's got a good relationship with his family and a gorgeous smile that never fails to make my own smile fill my face. He even held my chair out for me as I sat down. Ben is everything I should want, and yet, my heart doesn't flutter when he smiles at me. It doesn't change at all. My stomach doesn't tighten with anticipation of how he might find a way to touch my hand, or if he'll laugh at my jokes.

There's no chemistry whatsoever.

And to say I'm disappointed about that would be a huge understatement. All through our meal, I beg my libido to sit up and take notice. For my heart to start racing, or that warm tingle to start in the apex of my thighs.

But there's not a goddamn thing.

Despite our complete lack of chemistry, I'm determined to see this through. Ben's a nice guy and I need to get over Dom—even if just the thought of him makes my heart start to beat rapidly—so I laugh at Ben's jokes and tell him a little about my life. We commiserate about job challenges since we both work in corporate America. He talks about how close he is with his brother—Tessa's husband, Mike—and sister, Anna. I learn that he played baseball in college, but stopped after a knee injury. Now he coaches his nephew's T-ball team since his brother-in-law is deployed. In turn, I tell him about growing up as an only child and how desperately I wanted siblings. So bad that when I was six, I brought home my friend's little brother and told my parents he was now my little brother. Both sets of parents had a good laugh at my naivety. I tell him about my dad, and he reaches for my hand when I share that he died in a car accident. His touch is soothing, and another nail in our lack-of-chemistry coffin.

By the time dinner is over and he grabs the check, I'm trying hard to hide my disappointment that I haven't experienced even a single flutter of lust.

He pays for our dinner and then drives me back to my place. When we arrive, he opens the car door for me and then walks me inside with his hand resting on the middle of my back. It's a respectful touch, and I can't help wondering if this is what Dom would do at the end of a date. Or would his touch be lower, more intimate, and a little possessive.

I flush at the thought and fight the urge to literally shake these thoughts from my head.

I should not be thinking about Dom right now, I tell myself for the millionth time tonight. Maybe that's my problem. I spent too much time comparing Ben's actions to what Dom might do during the majority of our date. Maybe if I kiss Ben goodnight, that might spark something. Although I doubt a kiss will change our lack of chemistry, but I'll never know unless I try. It worked for Monica in that one episode of *Friends* when she kissed Pete. Maybe it can work for me too. A girl can hope.

Except when the elevator doors part on my floor, I see someone leaning against the wall near my door. Someone whose large frame I'd recognize anywhere.

Dom.

A swarm of butterflies takes off in my belly, and that elusive tingle between my thighs ignites like I just threw gasoline on a fire. But with all my lust comes anger. Why? Why now and not all night long when I was on a date with the perfect guy? Why is Dom the only man who makes my body light up like this? Who the hell in the universe did I piss off enough that my plight in life is to feel this way for the one man who doesn't feel the same?

Seriously, what the fuck, universe?

Dom's head turns at the sound of the elevator and he pushes off the wall, his light-blue eyes landing on me with an intensity that steals the breath from my lungs.

I've always thought Dom was attractive. He could be a doppelgänger for Jesse Williams, except even more fit and bulky. His eyes, though, have always been my favorite physical trait of his—a piercing aquamarine blue that never fails to ensnare me.

Seeing him after missing him these past three days is a confusing mix of relief and frustration, and it's becoming painfully apparent that those three days didn't make a damn bit of difference. I'm not sure any length of time will change how much I love him, and now I'm more convinced than ever that the universe is punishing me for something. And doing a damn fine job of it because this is fucking torture.

Dom's gaze slides over to the space next to me and then back to meet mine, a look I can't name in those crystal blues.

A clearing of a throat beside me grabs my attention, and I remember my date and the person Dom's gaze slid to.

Shit.

I break eye contact with Dom and reach for my keys in my purse while I try to pull myself together enough to not seem so affected. Obviously, this night isn't going to end the way I hoped it would.

EIGHT

Dominic

Who the fuck is this guy? And why the hell is he touching Laney?

My gaze flicks back to Laney, and that weird twisty sensation in my gut intensifies and my chest tightens. Fuck, she looks good. Her blonde hair falls in waves past her shoulders, and she's wearing a black dress that hugs every luscious curve. Her lips are coated with a deep-red lipstick that has my brain thinking thoughts I've never allowed myself to consider with her before. Like what they might feel like wrapped around my cock.

I swallow thickly and fight against the panic that's rising up until it feels like it's suffocating me. Wait. Is she on a date?

What the fuck? She tells me she's in love with me and then goes on a date with another guy?! Fuck no.

She rifles through her purse and then pulls out her keys. Her "date"—fuck, I hate him already for touching her, for thinking he has any right to her at all—drops his hand from her back when I glare at him.

His eyes widen. "Oh shit! You're Dominic Smith! Man,

I watched you play the other night against the Rams. You're a fucking legend!"

He extends his hand for me to shake. I glance to Alayna, who's staring at me with a furrow between her brows and that lush bottom lip tucked between her teeth. My gut warms with a desire I've never felt before—at least not this strongly since I've always been able to put her in the best friend box—and I reach out and shake her date's hand.

"Ben," he supplies his name even though I don't ask. He won't be around much longer for it to matter. There's no way she's dating this guy. He's not good enough for her. I don't know anything about him, but I'm sure of that much. No man is good enough for her.

He looks at Alayna, and his hand lands on her back again. I have to fight back a growl. I don't like him touching her, and I can finally admit to myself that it's not just because she's my best friend.

She is, but she's always been more than that.

Alayna is the kind of woman you commit to, which was something I'd promised myself I'd never do. I've never allowed myself to look at her as more than a friend because I knew I couldn't give her what she deserved, but being faced with the possibility of losing her completely has all my prior barriers dropping, and now I'm forced to see her—*really* see her.

She's fucking stunning, even as she shoots daggers at me for how rude I'm being to her date. But I'll take her anger over indifference any day. Anger means she still cares.

I've given her three days of space, but I can't stay away anymore. Not only do I miss the shit out of her, but Shawna is breathing down my throat about this fake relationship stunt. I came here to convince Laney to do this with me, and I'm more motivated than ever after seeing her walk down the hall with this ball bag. What would she have done if I wasn't standing here? Would she have let him kiss her? Would she have invited him in?

Red explodes through my vision at the thought of her with this guy.

No fucking way.

Not happening.

She belongs with me.

The thought is there before I'm fully aware of it, but the second it registers, my entire body goes on lockdown as my gaze shoots back to Laney, sliding down her tall, curvy frame.

How have I never noticed that she's fucking perfect? Her round ass that rivals any Kardashian and her thick thighs that I could grip firmly while I pound into her. She wouldn't be bony or cold like some of the women I've been with who cared more about their appearance than actually enjoying the act itself. No, Laney has always been passionate. She'd make sounds, maybe even scream as her thick thighs wrapped tight around my waist.

I suck in a sharp breath and come back to reality at the sound of my name.

Laney arches a brow. "Did you hear me?"

"No," I say, my voice hoarse. Her eyes narrow like she can't figure me out, which I'm thankful for. I'm also silently praying she doesn't look down because I can feel my hard dick pressing against the zipper of my dark wash jeans.

"I asked why are you here?"

"I need to talk to you." My voice sounds more normal, thank God.

She turns to Ben, her body separated by mere inches from his, and puts her hand on his bicep. "Thank you for tonight. I had a good time."

He smiles at her and I curl my hand into a fist. *I will not punch him. I will not punch him.*

"It was my pleasure." His gaze flicks to me before it lands back on her. "Maybe we can do it again sometime."

Her cheeks grow pink, and even from the side, I can see her give him her polite, composed smile. "Yeah, maybe."

Relief hits me hard. She doesn't want to go out with him again. Thank fuck.

Ben kisses her on the cheek, and I have to clench my jaw and swallow back the aggressive sound that wants to escape when his lips touch her skin. But then he walks away and she turns to me. The second her gaze connects with mine, Ben is forgotten.

There's that fire I love so much. That passion.

I'll process the change I'm feeling when it comes to her later when I'm alone. Right now, I'm just going to enjoy being near my best friend after three days apart and living in limbo, unsure if I'd be able to convince her to fight for our friendship. To fight for me.

But I know we'll be okay. Because even if she wants to give up, I'll never stop fighting for her.

My life is nothing without her in it. And I'll take her any way I can.

She huffs in exasperation and then opens her door and walks in, leaving it open for me to follow. I close it behind me and watch her, my gaze tracing every inch of her as she puts down her keys and purse on the side table and then slips out of her heels. She closes her eyes in bliss as her toes flex and then wanders over to the fridge to grab a bottle of water before moving to the couch. She tucks her legs under her as she sits, getting comfortable, and only then does she finally look at me.

Her lips part momentarily, and I wonder what she sees

in my eyes to get that reaction from her. Can she see the desire that's pulsing just underneath the surface? The sudden and intense hunger? I hope not. I know her well enough to know she wouldn't trust me if I confessed to feeling more than friendly feelings for her. She'd think I was doing it so she couldn't push me away.

So I reel in the new, confusing feelings swirling inside me and sit down on the other side of her couch. I spin so I'm facing her and then pause when I see the hurt look on her face. There's still anger too, but I can read Laney like the most interesting book in the world. And I can recognize hurt in her gaze.

"Why were you on a date with that guy?"

"What do you mean?"

"I mean, you confessed that you were in love with me only three days ago and now you're on a date with another guy?" I can't hide the accusation in my tone, but hopefully it covers the hurt buried underneath.

Her cheeks flush. "Are you fucking serious right now? I told you I needed space. And if I recall correctly, when I told you about my feelings, you completely ignored them and had the audacity to ask me to be your fake girlfriend."

I stare at her, at a loss for words. She's not wrong. I can admit I didn't exactly handle that situation well, but I'm still trying to fully wrap my head around her confession—hell, about my own emerging feelings that I'm starting to realize have been under the surface for a lot longer than I wanted to admit.

Apparently I'm silent too long because she rolls her eyes, shoves off the couch, and stomps back to the door before ripping it open. "Can we make this the last time you show up on my doorstep unannounced? I need space to think, Dom. And you need to leave. I'll call you when I'm ready."

"And how long will that be?" I ask as I stand up, not wanting to leave but also not wanting to piss her off even more.

Her eyes turn sad for a moment, and my gut clenches even as a sharp pain jabs my heart. "I don't know," she says, her voice low and losing the anger and frustration. But then she rolls her shoulders back and gestures for me to leave.

I don't know what to do, so I do what she's asking and walk out. But I stop as soon as I get to the threshold and look down at her, capturing her gaze and hoping she can see all the sincerity in mine.

"You're the only person in my life who matters, Laney. I'll prove it to you."

And then I leave, feeling even more unsure about where we stand than I was when I came here.

NINE

Alayna

I lean back on my stool to get a better look of the painting on my easel. I lift what's left of my glass of wine—okay, it's my second—and take a sip, staring at the piece before me.

"Holy shit," Tessa murmurs next to me. Her eyes are glued to my painting, her own paintbrush held frozen in her hand. "Why the hell are you a data analyst when you can paint like that?"

She acts almost offended and I fight hard not to laugh. This isn't the first time we've come to Paint & Pinot, or the first time she's been awed by how my painting turned out.

"Okay, but seriously. I know you always brush me off, but *come on.*" She gestures to my painting. "You could sell that for thousands. You're *that* good. Why would you want to be stuck in a stuffy corporate office?"

I put my paintbrush down and take another sip of my wine. "I'm good at my job."

It's a weak excuse, which is only confirmed when Tessa arches her brow in a *get real* look. The truth is a lot more complicated, but the wine has loosened my inhibitions enough that I open up to her, sharing something only Dom knows.

"When my dad died, my mom fell apart. I think he was the only man she's ever loved." It's a big reason I haven't cut her out of my life. I get why she is the way she is—it's her protective mechanism. She became a shallow version of herself and goes through men like bubble gum because it keeps her from getting her heart too broken. The problem is Mom doesn't just keep her men at arm's length, but everyone, me included.

"She'd also relied on him for everything, which hadn't seemed like a big deal when I was little, but after he died, she struggled a lot financially, until one day, about a year after my dad died, she just flipped the switch. It was like the one-year mark came and she turned off her grief, but in doing so her entire personality changed. She started dating super-rich guys. I didn't even know how she was meeting them because we lived in a small town, but then I figured out she'd befriended someone who lived in one of the wealthier towns about an hour away. They'd basically hunt down these rich, eligible bachelors to provide for them. These guys would wine and dine her, buy her extravagant gifts, and she grew really accustomed to that lifestyle, but it wasn't one she knew how to replicate without them, so she got stuck in this vicious cycle of dependency. Now, she's completely reliant on whichever man she's dating. She has nothing for herself. If they drop her, she's scrambling to find the next one to provide for her. I watched her do this enough times that I promised myself I'd never rely on a man to provide for me, which meant finding a stable job."

She nods in understanding. "Like being a data analyst when you could be a huge artist."

I scoff. "I think you're exaggerating my talents."

"I'm not. Alayna, I know this is just supposed to be amateur hour while we do something fun and drink lots of wine, but you're seriously talented. Has no one ever told you that before?"

My dad did. All the time, in fact. Dom has too, but he learned long ago not to push me about it.

Watching my mom was a lesson in life I couldn't ignore, no matter how much I loved painting. And I wasn't lying when I said I was good at my job. It's why I get paid six figures a year with crazy-good benefits. Stanley—our boss— knows my value to our company. Sometimes it's okay for a hobby to be just that, even if people think you're really good at it. I love painting. It relaxes me and gives me a creative outlet working with numbers all day never could. But the pressure of doing it for a living would probably stress me out to the point where all my creativity would freeze up, and the idea of living in panic about how or where my next paycheck would be coming from is enough to make me tremble in my seat.

Tessa shakes her head sadly. "God, what a waste. I bet there are millionaires all over the world who would kill to have your paintings in their mansions."

"Eh, I'll keep them to myself."

She lets out an overly dramatic sigh, and I finish off my wine while fighting back a smile. I love her, and I get that not everyone likes their corporate job, but I'm content with my life. Most of it anyway. I can pay all my bills and have extra money for savings and for fun. I don't need anyone to provide for me or make sure I have everything I need.

I do all that myself.

It might be a little lonely at times, but at least it's safe. I know I'll never get the rug ripped out from under me.

Tessa stares at her own painting and takes another drink of her wine. "Do you ever think about how your life might be different if your dad hadn't died and your mom hadn't become...well, how she is now?"

Ah, reflective Tessa. Whenever we drink, she becomes reflective one drink before she becomes comedic gold and two drinks before she's straight-up drunk.

"Not really. What's the point?"

It's the truth, although some probably think it's weird I never think about what my life might've been like if things hadn't happened the way they did. Especially with how long I've been playing the what if game with my relationship with Dom.

What if he finally noticed me as more than his best friend?

What if he fell in love with me?

What if...

And on it would go. Yet, I rarely had those thoughts when it came to my family.

"Really?" she asks.

"Maybe because I accepted a long time ago that nothing was going to change. My dad wasn't coming back to life, and while my mom could've changed, it got to a point where I realized she never would."

She watches me for a minute, a sad look on her face. "I think you set your expectations low so you won't get hurt."

I reel back. "Where did that come from?"

"Face it, Alayna. I love you, but you settle for a life of mediocrity because it's stable and reliable, but boring as hell."

"My life isn't boring." Is it?

Tessa arches a brow and I frown. I mean, yeah, okay,

most of my excitement comes from things I do with Dom because he's a big shot—like our annual trip to somewhere tropical and relaxing—but I do other things that are interesting and fun without him. Things I can't think of off the top of my head but I'm sure I have some. My entire life isn't *only* about stable and reliable.

My job is, yes, but that's not abnormal. Plenty of people work boring day jobs.

And so what if I keep my friends group small? Quality over quantity.

And okay, maybe this wine night is the first night I've had out since Dom's birthday, but that's because I've been busy with work and then tired at night, and I like to be in bed no later than ten so I get a good night's rest, and...

Oh my God, she's right.

My jaw goes slack as I stare at her and try to rack my brain for any example that proves her wrong, but I draw a complete blank.

She nibbles her lip and then frowns sympathetically. "Sorry. I think I've had too much to drink."

She sets her wine glass down even though there's still wine left in it, but it's too late now. She's passed off her introspective state to me, and suddenly I'm not feeling all that proud of the life I've built. All my excitement and most of my fun comes from hanging out with Dom and his friends.

What do I have without that?

Wine nights with Tessa are fun, but that's not enough, is it?

For the first time since I made the decision to cut Dom out of my life, I'm realizing I don't know who I am anymore without him. I may not have been dependent on him financially, but I'm starting to fear that there are other ways to depend on someone that might be equally unhealthy.

Maybe it's time I started figuring out who I am on my own.

TEN

Dominic

I'm not a guy who pines for a woman. I've never felt more than a passing interest in getting laid and being done with the whole thing. The fewer strings the better. I never felt lonely or felt like I was lacking anything in my life.

I'm quickly realizing that's because I had Laney.

Through all the women, the family drama, the crazy travel schedules—there was always Laney waiting for me when I wanted to just hang out and let my guard down. When I wanted to laugh or talk about something deeper than the latest celebrity gossip or football.

Laney's absence has created a vast emptiness in my life that I've never experienced before, and I'm man enough to admit I'm not handling it well.

Even as the press continues to hound me over Jen Summers, and Shawna calls every fucking day asking about my mystery woman and reminding me we need to get this plan in action as soon as possible.

None of it makes me feel anything.

I come home every day—if I even leave—to an empty house and my fingers twitching to pick up my phone and call Laney, just to hear her huff and yell at me for not giving her space.

Fuck, what I'd give to have her yell at me right now. Any excuse for her to talk to me, to be in the same room with me.

My phone dings, and I glance down to find another unsaved number inviting me to some Hollywood party tonight. I've got a dozen invites just like it, but not a single one interests me. None of these people are the one person I really want to hang out with.

My chest aches and I rub it absentmindedly while I stare out at my pool and perfectly manicured backyard. I pay a lot of money to keep it maintained. Normally, looking out at what my career has paid for makes me feel on top of the world, but nothing can pull me out of the hole I've dug for myself.

I move away from the floor-to-ceiling window and plop down on the couch, grabbing the remote in a lame attempt at distraction. I'm also hoping noise from the TV might help lessen the silence and loneliness that seem to permeate every corner of my house.

After twenty minutes of mindless channel surfing and not feeling any closer to clarity, I shut off the TV.

Fuck, how did this become my life? We go to the biggest game in the league next week, and I'm sitting on my couch moping over a woman.

Not just any woman, though. *The* woman.

How did I seriously never notice it before? Never appreciate her the way she deserved? It's been a long time since I reflected on my life and the choices I've made to get here. I'm not sure I've taken a deep look at my life since I was in high school and my world was rocked by my dad's betrayal.

But I would do it now—for Laney. If figuring out where I'd gone wrong would help me fix things between us, I'd do it, no matter how uncomfortable it made me to face up to the mistakes I'd made.

I would do anything for her.

I look around my huge living room with the ten-foot ceilings and open floor plan. The grays and whites don't give it any personality, but it's what the interior designer I hired recommended. It never felt this cold and bare before, did it?

The only change is Laney's not here or planning to come over, and once again I'm realizing another way I took her for granted. I didn't just take for granted the things she organized for me—like my birthday party—but also the way she brought warmth to my life. Her presence alone added to my life in a way that can't be replaced by the sound of a TV or material items. It can only be filled by Laney's laughter, her teasing, her shoes resting on the floor at the end of the coffee table while she tucks her legs underneath her and tells me about her day.

Fuck, I miss her.

The doorbell rings and I debate ignoring it, but after the third ring, I push myself off the couch and make my way to the door.

I shouldn't be surprised to see Shawna on the other side, but I am.

She pushes her way past me into my house. "You've been ignoring me, and I have half a mind to fire you and tell you to find a new, better PR person, but I'm the best and your situation intrigues me. So let's cut to the chase. Why are you avoiding me? Is it about this mystery woman you said you had? Let me guess, she's not real."

My shoulders tense as my defenses rise. "She's real. I've

just run into some roadblocks in getting her to agree to do this."

Her eyes narrow. "Explain."

So I do—because whether I like it or not, I did get myself into a mess, and Shawna's right that she's the best in the business. She doesn't say anything while I speak, but she does occasionally jot down a note or two in a small notebook she pulls from her oversized purse.

"So, if I understand correctly, you still stand by your original position that you won't do this unless"—she looks down at her notes—"Alayna Pritchard does it with you. Is that correct?"

"Yeah."

She stands up from the stool she was sitting on. "Alright. I'll be in touch. And the next time I call, Dom, you better answer."

"Yes, ma'am."

She walks out of my house with purpose and her phone already to her ear. I'm a little terrified of what she's planning, and I doubt she's going to change course just because Laney refuses to be my partner. But I still refuse to do this with anyone but her, and for more reasons than I initially had.

ELEVEN

Alayna

No one ever suggests that journeys of self-discovery are often fraught with a lot of things you don't like. I didn't have any Elizabeth Gilbert moments of deep perspective-finding; *Eat, Pray, Love* my journey was not.

Maybe I still could, but after a week of "exploring" and trying to have fun on my own, the only real thing I discovered was that I loved my alone time and my independent hobbies, like painting.

People can be really overwhelming—and that's saying something when I'm used to the football crowd.

I did all the things you see in movies.

I tried yoga—and somehow fell asleep in child's pose and woke up with a snort because I'd fallen into such a deep sleep I was snoring and drooling on my yoga mat.

So yoga's out because I'll never show my face there again.

I tried going out to eat by myself at a nice restaurant that I've been wanting to try. Things were going fine until the elderly couple beside me decided that it was too sad for "such a beautiful young woman to be dining alone" and then promptly spent the rest of dinner showing me pictures of their grandson who was my age and was quite a catch— their words not mine.

I tried joining a bowling league because bowling always seems like a fun idea. I was kicked off when my thumb got stuck on the release and the ball ended up popping off my hand. Instead of flying down my lane like I'd hoped, the momentum of my body and my swing caused the ball to cross three other lanes and for everyone around me to glare at me in reproach. Yeah, no. I was not repeating that ever again.

My last attempt was going on a hike. Getting close to nature always seems like a good idea in movies, but I came home with a minor sunburn and itching like crazy in what turned out to be poison ivy. Needless to say, it confirmed that I'm not an outdoorsy girl. Put me in a tropical paradise and I'll relax under a palm tree with a mimosa in hand. Put me in the wilderness and it's a completely different story.

But despite failing spectacularly at all those individual things, the week wasn't a complete bust because it had taught me one very valuable lesson.

I could do things on my own. I wasn't lost without Dom. I missed him, but my world didn't revolve around him in the same way I'd always thought it had. I now knew with a certainty I hadn't possessed before that failing at something —whether it was yoga, dinner for one, hiking, or anything else I deemed to try in the future—wasn't a failure. It was a lesson. It was trial and error to find what I liked or didn't. I could have fun by myself.

Apart from that, I also met people I never would've met before, like the waitress who commiserated with me after the elderly couple finally left. Apparently they were regulars who tried to pawn their grandson off on everyone. We got to talking, and it must've been all the wine I was drinking but I confessed to painting on the side and even showed her a couple of pictures I'd snapped on my phone of paintings I'd done. Turns out, her uncle owns an art gallery here in LA, and now I'm on my way to meet with him.

I haven't told a soul. I can only imagine the shriek Tessa would produce if she heard I was going to show an actual art professional my paintings. I doubt anything will come of it, but my motto this week has been to say yes. Yes to new experiences, yes to new opportunities, no matter how uncomfortable they make me.

And talking about my art makes me extremely uncomfortable.

I arrive at the gallery a few minutes early and take a deep, steadying breath. My stomach is in knots as I grab a few of my canvases. Very few people have seen these, but they're a few of my favorites. Despite the fear stiffening my muscles, I walk toward the door and push it open. A small bell dings, and a man calls out from a back room.

"Be out in a minute."

I stand awkwardly in the middle of the room, looking around at the artwork on the walls. One wall is full of portraits that look like photographs, but on closer inspection, I discover they're drawings. My stomach tightens even more with imposter syndrome. My paintings aren't nearly as good as those.

Along another wall, there are painted landscapes that are done in watercolors, and yet they appear vibrant and bold. Sunsets, night scenes, and a beautiful sunrise over a mountaintop that has me staring wide-eyed.

A deep voice startles me. "Like those?"

I snap my gaze to meet his. He's much older than I am, and if I had to guess he's closer to his fifties, but still in good shape. His blue eyes sparkle as he smiles. "Cat got your tongue?"

I give him a bashful smile. "Sorry. They're beautiful." I gesture to all the work in the room because I couldn't pick a favorite to save my life.

He looks around, pride visible in his gaze as he settles his hands on his hips in a look that on others might seem like they don't know what to do with their hands, but on him comes off as relaxed.

"I've been fortunate to showcase some great talent." His discerning gaze comes back to me and glances down at the canvases in my arms. "I'm Jared. My niece spoke very highly of you."

My cheeks flush with a blush. "I've never really showed my work to many people," I admit. "I might've only had the courage to show her because I'd had slightly too much wine."

The corner of his mouth tilts up in a small smile. "Well, let's see if we can put those negative thoughts to rest, hmm?"

I nod, although now the tightness in my stomach has turned into a sharp nausea that has me struggling to breathe as I lift the canvases and place them on the table he gestures to. He doesn't say a word as he lays them out and then looks them over, his gaze serious and focused. I nibble on my thumb before I realize what I'm doing and then drop it to my side. I shouldn't be nervous. It doesn't matter if he loves them or hates them. I have a job. I don't need my art to be seen by the masses or sold or—

"These are spectacular," he says as he turns that sharp gaze to me. There's almost a hint of accusation in it like he doesn't trust why I was so nervous, but that also might be me projecting.

"Thank you," I murmur.

That hint of a smile makes another appearance and then he stands tall. "Tell you what. I just had an artist vacate, so I've got room if you'd like to put these up for display. We can negotiate the price, but the gallery will take a partial commission."

My head spins. "Wait. Are you serious? You want to sell these?"

"Yeah. That's why you're here, right?"

"To be honest, I figured you'd tell me they were great for amateur stuff and send me on my way."

His smile grows. "Alayna, I can assure you these are definitely great and not at all something I'd consider 'amateur stuff.'"

I open and close my mouth like a gaping fish, trying to wrap my head around what he's telling me. The whole time he just continues to smile a knowing smile like he's used to this kind of reaction—and maybe he is.

I can't believe he really wants to put up my artwork for sale—*my* artwork. What is even happening right now?

"I can see you're reeling, so how about you go home and think it over. If you've got more like these, I'll gladly take those too. You're very talented, Alayna, and I have no doubt this will be a lucrative partnership for us both, if you're up for it."

"Um...I...yeah, thinking on it would be good," I say, stumbling over my words. This is surreal.

It's not until I get back in my car that his offer hits me with the full force of a linebacker. He wants to sell my art, and more than that, he thinks it'll actually make us some money.

I don't know if I'm brave enough to take him up on his offer, but a big part of me wants to, and if there's anything

I've learned this last week, it's that doing scary things can sometimes be really rewarding.

Maybe I've been looking at this art thing wrong the whole time. Maybe it's possible to have both a career that I'm good at and make some side money off my art. I don't have to sacrifice one or the other.

For the first time in weeks, I feel hopeful and excited about what the future holds.

By the time I get home, I've already decided I'm going to partner with Jared and let him try to sell my art. I'm all about taking chances now and this feels like a potentially really rewarding one. I'm on cloud nine as I get settled in comfy clothes and get to work on a new art piece. I have work in the morning so I can't stay up too late, but I've got a ton of ideas and one in particular that I really want to get down on canvas. I've got everything set up when there's a knock on my door.

My stomach feels like it's doing somersaults as I walk over to it. Is it Dom again? I can't decide if I'd be happy or frustrated if it is him. So far, he's been respecting my space edict, but it's been over a week now since we talked, which is the longest we've ever gone without speaking, and I hate to say it, but I miss him.

I peek out the peephole and pause when I see it's a woman. I open the door and take in the stranger who's dressed in an elegant pantsuit—or as elegant as a pantsuit can be. Her hair is swept back in a chignon, and on her face is a smile that is just shy of authentic.

"Are you Alayna Pritchard?"

"Yes. Can I help you?"

"Actually, you can. May I come in?"

"Not until you tell me who you are and why I should let you."

Her smile grows and this time it's real. "I can see why he wants you."

I frown. "Excuse me?"

She extends her hand. "I'm Shawna Cramer. I'm Dom's new PR rep."

My shoulders sag. "Did he send you?"

"Actually, I suspect he'd rip me a new one if he knew I was here, but I figured we could talk woman to woman."

Reluctantly, I open the door and let her in. She walks in with her head held regally high, and her gaze sweeps over my apartment. There's a thoughtful expression on her face that makes me wonder what she's thinking, but I don't ask.

"Would you like some water? I don't have much else to drink," I ask her.

"No, thank you. I'd prefer to not waste time and get down to it."

"Alright," I say, dragging the word because I'm still not entirely sure why she's here.

"Dom told me that he wanted you for this plan we've got in place. Do you know what I'm talking about?"

"You mean the fake relationship that's supposed to help his image."

She smiles and it's back to that fake smile. "It will absolutely help his image. These sorts of things always do as long as both parties behave."

"I already told him no," I say, crossing my arms over my chest because suddenly it feels like a chill has filled the room.

"I know. That's what he told me. But he's refusing to do this with anyone else, and he needs this, Alayna. His reputation is shit right now. Jen Summers is having a field day with the press and crying on cue about how heartbroken she is over the whole thing." She rolls her eyes, and I warm to her a little because clearly she thinks Jen's full of shit.

"So what do you need from me?"

She watches me thoughtfully before pulling a folder from her oversized purse and moving to my kitchen table. "I need your help picking one of these women for Dom. You know him best, according to him. You'll be able to tell me which one he might consider replacing you with because we need to get started on this ASAP."

I walk cautiously over to the table and see pictures of five women, each famous in their own right. I see a senator's daughter, another Hollywood starlet, an heiress, a very popular singer, and a celebrity chef. I glance at the sheet next to each photo which has a breakdown of their strengths and why they'd be a good match. Some information has clearly been left out, and I'm only vaguely aware of a few of the scandals that would cause them to want to participate in an arrangement like this.

But I don't need any of that information to know none will be a good pick for Dom. The senator's daughter will remind him too much of the cheerleader he hooked up with in college who stalked him when he didn't agree to date her. The Hollywood starlet is a known cokehead, and Dom doesn't fuck around with people who do drugs. The heiress is a ditzy bimbo—which I hate saying about any woman, but is painfully true after I met her once—who will drive Dom crazy after thirty seconds. I thought I heard a rumor that the celebrity chef threatened to cut off her fiancé's balls and has three different restraining orders on her. The only one who's got potential is the singer. She's gorgeous, popular, and would no doubt look great standing next to him, but staring at her picture doesn't make me see anything but a haze of green.

I don't want him to be paired up with these women. Not a single one will have his back; I know that much. They'll be in it for themselves, and Dom needs someone who will look out for him.

"None of these women will work."

She frowns and comes closer, looking down at the folders with me. "Are you sure? We really need to get moving on this. With the Super Bowl only a week away, we've got to find someone soon so we can get him some positive press before the season ends and his coaches don't have a daily reminder of how good he is on the field and why they need to keep him."

Fuck, she's right. His time to save his spot on the team is running out, and there's nothing Dom loves more than playing with Gabe, Ty, and Romel for the Wolves.

I had my reasons for not wanting to be part of this charade, but I've also had time away from Dom, time for myself, and that time has given me some perspective. I thought I wasn't strong enough to pretend for six months, but I know better now. I can do this. I can be his person—one last time.

"I'll do it."

TWELVE

Dominic

"The plan is pretty straightforward. You need to be seen in public, cozying up together, holding hands, that sort of thing. Don't make any comment to the press. We want them to be salivating and speculating, and then we'll release a statement about how you've been there for Dom through all his ups and downs and he finally saw what was right in front of him. One thing led to another, and now here you are."

I glance over at Laney, who is staring at Shawna with a blank expression. My stomach is in knots. I'm usually a pretty self-assured guy, but ever since Alayna tried to end our friendship, I feel like I've been on thin ice, just one step away from falling through. I don't like it at all.

And that was before she confessed to being in love with me.

Shawna continues to yammer on about the plan—one I've already heard before—but I struggle to pay attention, instead continuing to slide my glance to Laney. She's wearing a pink sweater that I remember her buying last year. But I don't remember it hugging her breasts the way it is now. My mouth goes dry as my gaze peruses my best friend, noticing things about her I never have before. Like how her hair falls in golden waves to her shoulders, or how her blue eyes have flecks of darker blue close to the black. I've always noticed how she nibbles the inside of her lip—like she's doing right now—when she's unsure, but it's never caused such a visceral reaction on my body before.

I subtly shift in my chair and discreetly adjust my now semi-hard dick. Reaching forward, I grab the water bottle that Shawna's assistant put out for us and take a hearty swallow. I need to pull my shit together. Laney doesn't need another reason to drop me like a bad habit.

What would she do if she caught me getting hard for her after she confessed her feelings for me and I sat there like a bump on a log, too stunned to say anything?

But despite my pep talk to get my dick under control, I spend the rest of the meeting fighting the urge to pull her bottom lip from her teeth with my thumb and watch her eyes widen as I lean forward and take it between my own.

Yeah, that doesn't help my boner situation either.

Finally, Shawna claps her hands together, then folds them and rests them along the table as she leans on her elbows, excitement glittering in her eyes. "Any questions?"

Alayna doesn't glance my way. "And this is only for six months, right?"

Shawna's gaze flicks to me at the same time that my eyes widen, silently pleading with her to say yes.

She focuses back on Alayna. "Unless you'd be willing to negotiate those terms..."

Alayna sits up a little taller. "You mean, like less time. Maybe three months instead?" She sounds so hopeful, bile rises in my throat. Can she really not stand to be around me anymore?

Shawna's worth her weight in gold and doesn't skip a beat. "Unfortunately, no. I was thinking longer. The more time we can carry this on, the better. We really need the public to believe it. Plus, the longer this goes on, the less likely the team will trade him."

Alayna's shoulders drop and she nods to herself. "Right," she mumbles. "Alright. Then I guess we get started today?" Still, she doesn't look at me.

Shawna perks up. "Today would be perfect. The sooner we can get the press talking about you two, the better. I've got a list of options for dates for the next week. Why don't I leave you two to pick one for today and then we'll get everything set up on our end and get some others scheduled for you."

Laney frowns. "Set up how?"

Shawna smiles like she thinks Laney is adorably naive. "We're the ones who tell the press when and where they need to be. You don't think most of those celeb photos are just luck, do you? Those are staged. Welcome to fame, sweetie. Enjoy the ride." Without another word, she grabs her stack of papers, leaving one behind with a breakdown of some of our options for tonight, then leaves the room.

"You've talked me into a lot of crazy stuff, Dom, but this really takes the cake." She picks up the paper and starts silently reading down the list.

I can't explain it, but a pressure grows in my chest as I stare at the side of her face. I need her eyes on me. I need to see those cerulean blues and get lost in them like I have so many times—more times than she'll ever know. Reaching over, I place my hand over hers, and her gaze snaps to mine.

There she is. Fire, ice, and everything between. She's the most beautiful and complex woman I've ever known.

My shoulders ease, and that reliefs flows down my body like I just stepped into a hot shower.

"Thank you," I say, watching her eyes soften and her lips part to speak, but I keep going. "I know you don't want to do this, but there's no one else I could be this vulnerable with."

A little wrinkle forms between her brows. "It's all fake, Dom. You don't have to be vulnerable at all."

I squeeze her hand. "You know I'm a shit actor. I'd have to have real conversations, and that could mean exposing things I don't want to and having to spend an excessive amount of time with a stranger. If I'm going to spend time outside of football with anyone, it's you."

She gets a look in her eyes—one she's gotten before, but I can never figure out what it means—and swallows thickly. "You can be a real asshole, you know," she says, her voice soft.

"I know."

"And then you go and say something like that and it's hard to stay mad at you."

I smile weakly.

"But make no mistake. I want to stay mad at you. I *need* to." Now it's my turn to frown in confusion, but she continues. "And when this is all said and done, you'll have the Wolves, and I'll move on. Got it?"

"If that's still what you want in six months, then I'll respect that."

It's a lie. The first one I've told her in a long time, but I don't regret it because I'll do whatever it takes to make sure when we hit that six-month mark, she's still by my side and we're stronger than ever.

I let Laney choose our "date" which is eating dinner at an exclusive restaurant on the beach. She's always loved the beach. When we both moved to California, she dragged me straight to the closest one she could find, kicked off her shoes, and dug her toes into the sand. I can still remember it as clearly as if it happened yesterday. The way she tilted her head back, her hair—longer then—falling nearly to her round ass. The corners of her pale pink lips tilted in a wide smile and her eyes closed as she soaked in the warmth of the California sun. I couldn't take my eyes off her. She radiated pure happiness, and I wanted to relish in her simple joy.

Things were easier back then, both of us fresh out of college and excited about the future. I never told her how relieved I was when she announced she'd gotten a job in Los Angeles and would be moving with me. She doesn't know that I'd spent weeks fighting against the panic of being separated from her. Our friendship had never been challenged by long distance, apart from me being gone for away games. I was afraid that if we weren't in each other's orbit, she'd build a life where I no longer fit.

Thinking back on those early days in California, I can't help wondering when I let things derail so much. When did I start choosing parties and overrated celebrities over my best friend?

And is there any way to get us back to the way things used to be? Or is she right, and we've grown too far apart?

No. Laney and I can get through anything. Our friendship is stronger than my fuckups. I just have to convince her of that. I have to convince her it can be even more.

The waiter seats us at a table on the balcony where there's a clear view of the beach and a group of paparazzi already waiting for us. Laney stares at them for a moment, and I wish more than anything she'd tell me what thoughts are circling in that brain of hers. There was a time when we had no secrets from each other, and I wouldn't even have to ask to know what she was thinking.

But now I question if that's really true since she had a pretty big secret she never told me before—her feelings for me.

She turns to me and pastes on the fakest smile I've ever seen her wear. My jaw clenches before she even speaks, hating the distance I've put between us—because I'm not dumb enough to blame this distance on her when it's my own damn fault she's acting this way. "Guess it's time to put on a show," she says.

I shrug, feigning a nonchalance I don't feel. "Or we could just be us."

Her smile stiffens like it's taking everything for her to keep it on her face and not frown. "Not if we're trying to sell that we're a couple."

"Why not? People used to assume that about us all the time. How many people from high school kept asking if we were finally dating?"

Her smile falls this time, and I almost wish it was back—even as fake as it was—because the hurt in her eyes before she drops her gaze to the table feels like being sucker punched. I reach over and grab her hand. "Hey, talk to me. Please," I tack on, needing her to let me in.

She shakes her head and then looks up at me, her eyes guarded. "You don't get it, Dom." She leans forward and lowers her voice. "You think this is easy for me? I confessed my feelings for you, and you're treating it like it's not a big deal. Like I should be totally fine 'faking it' when I used to dream about moments like this." She pulls her hand from mine and reaches for her water, taking a long drink. Her features soften as she places it back on the table, and that fake smile is planted firmly back on her face. "Let's just get this night over with, okay?"

The waiter arrives to take our order, but I ask for a few more minutes since I haven't even bothered to look over the menu. I've been too distracted by the woman sitting in front of me who I used to know so well and now feels like a complete stranger.

She looks down at her menu, but I can't just ignore the comment she made. "I didn't mean to imply this was easy for you. It's not easy for me either." I lean closer. "Laney, you're my best friend and the most important person in my life. You think it's easy to know I've fucked up so badly that you can hardly look at me? That you've only given me fake smiles since we got here? That you've put an end date on our friendship and I'm trying my hardest not to panic the fuck out over the idea of losing you completely? It's not easy for me either. The only thing easy—the reason you were the only person I would agree to do this with—is spending time with you. I'm not ignoring your feelings or what you confessed. But you dropped a bomb on me, and I'm still processing. Can I process and still have a good time with you?"

Her brows are furrowed, and she's got this cute little wrinkle above her nose. "What? You want me to just compartmentalize my feelings so we can laugh it up and pretend like everything's fine? Like you didn't ditch me at *your* birthday party for some Hollywood starlet and cause the scandal of your career."

"Okay," I say, wanting to make sure she doesn't add more to the list of my faults—we both know that list could be a mile long. "Let's start there. Clearly you're pissed about what happened, so let's talk about it."

She looks around the half-full restaurant before

focusing back on me. "We can't talk about that here. We're supposed to be cozying up and looking like we're happy. If we talk about that, I'm only going to get pissed all over again."

"Then get pissed. Get fucking pissed at me, Laney. Because this"—I gesture to her body and face—"this version of you is fake, and I didn't pick you so that our conversations could be as fake as a porn star's tits."

She rolls her eyes. "Lovely image there, Dom."

"Let me have it. Give me the real Laney."

Her jaw moves back and forth like she's chewing her words, and then she unleashes, and even though every word is like being cut with glass, it feels so good to see that fire back in her eyes that I'd take it all night long.

"Fine. You want the truth. I felt used and worthless after that party. I've felt that way for months. You only want me when I can do something for you. This whole arrangement, for example. You don't care about anyone's feelings but your own. And I can't pinpoint when you became this person, but I *hate* this version of you. You're such a selfish dickhead, I want nothing to do with you. Is that what you want to hear? That, as in love with you as I've always been, I can't stand to be near you anymore? Well, there you go. There's the whole fucking truth. I hate Jen Summers, even though she's drop-dead gorgeous, so I totally get your infatuation with her, but that night was supposed to be us partying together. *Us* celebrating your birthday, not you ditching me to go have sex."

She swallows and that fire rages in her eyes, even as they glisten and her voice shakes. "I hate that I love you. I hate that even after you continue to hurt me, I still wish you wanted me the way I've wanted you. I hate being this vulnerable with you when you've done nothing to deserve it. I hate that somewhere along the road I forgot who I was without you and now I need to figure it out because I can't keep doing this, Dom. I can't keep being your wingwoman that you keep in the shadows unless it serves you. So this is the last thing you get from me. Understand?"

THIRTEEN

Alayna

My heart races and my eyes sting from holding back the tears that threaten to build, but this man has taken enough away from me at this point that I refuse to give him my tears too. He stares at me, his mouth parting slightly before he closes it again and something akin to agony fills those crystalline-blue eyes.

"Are we ready to order?" The waiter pops up out of nowhere, and I cover my surprise by looking down at my menu and pointing to something random. "I'll have this." I don't even know what I ordered, but I don't care. I need to pull myself together. Everything I told him was true, even if I'm not entirely upset about figuring out who I am without him. It's been enlightening and something I probably should've invested time in long before now.

The waiter glances at Dom, his pen poised above his notepad, but Dom's gaze is locked on me. "She'll have the bacon-wrapped filet mignon, and I'll have the grilled chicken."

He hands the menu to the waiter, who remains frozen next to our table. My eyes are focused on Dom who doesn't look anywhere but at me. I didn't even realize they had bacon-wrapped filet mignon here, and even though I'm a little peeved he ordered for me, I also love steak.

"Um...are you sure you don't want the stuffed tomato?" the waiter asks me, his eyes wide as saucers, unsure if he should take Dom's order for both of us.

Wait...I ordered *a tomato*? I hate tomatoes.

"Uh, yeah. The filet will be great. Thanks." I hand the waiter my menu and he scurries away.

Dom's eyes soften when I look back over at him, and the corner of his lips tilt up ever so slightly. But then his expression sobers. "I'm sorry," he says, his voice low but clear. "You'll never know how much, but I'm sorry for how I've treated you. I'm ashamed of a lot of the things I've done, but I'm most ashamed that I've made you feel like you mean less than the whole world to me."

I swallow thickly. "You can't sweet talk me now and expect that to make everything better."

"I don't. I expect you to keep calling me out when I'm being an ass. As long as you don't expect me to give up on saving our friendship before my six months are up because I won't. That's the one thing you can't ask me to do."

We're silent as we watch each other before I finally say, "You were wrong."

"About what?"

"You said I mean the whole world to you, but that's not true. It's never been true. Football means more." His brows furrow and his lips turn down. "It's okay, Dom. I've always known my place in your life. But I don't want you to pretend I hold a higher status than I do. I think it's time we were both realistic."

He shakes his head twice. "Clearly I have a lot more work cut out for me than I realized."

I'm not sure what he means by that, and I'm afraid to ask. So I don't.

•

A tabloid is thrown on my desk, a picture of Dom and me sitting at our table the other night. His expression looks almost hungry—for something other than food—but I know the truth. That was when he told me he wasn't going to give up on our friendship. His determination—and stubbornness—is legendary. The headline is in big bold letters above the image. *Dominic Smith scores new lady—Jen Summers forgotten?*

I fight back a roll of my eyes and glance up at Tessa, whose perfectly trimmed brow is arched high. "Mind filling me in? I thought you were done with him?"

I blow out a breath and lean back in my chair. "It's not what it looks like."

I didn't think it was possible but her brow arches higher. "Really? Cause it looks like you were on a date with him."

I can't tell her the truth. Not that I don't trust her, but that was part of the agreement I signed with Dom's new PR person.

Leaning forward, I rub circles on my temples, hoping to stem the headache that's been growing ever since I agreed to this stupid idea.

"I told him," I confess.

"That you wanted to end your friendship?"

"That too."

Her eyes go wide and she inhales sharply. "You *told* him?"

I nod and fight back a laugh as she drops in the chair on the other side of my desk, looking at me like she doesn't know me at all. "I can't believe you told him and are just now telling me. We've been at work for hours! How did he take it? Was this at dinner?" she asks, pointing to the picture of us on the front page of the tabloid. "Tell me everything!"

"It was before that. It was a few weeks ago, actually."

"So the dinner really was a date!" She sits up tall and looks like she's about to start clapping like a peppy cheerleader, which I can't have because there's honestly nothing to cheer about.

But I also can't tell her that everything she's going to witness for the next six months is completely fake.

How the hell did this become my life?

"It was just a trial thing. You know Dom's not really a commitment guy." Understatement of the century.

Her eyes narrow. "Why aren't you ecstatic about this? You've been pining for this guy for as long as I've known you, and now he's finally stepping up and you seem...I don't know, almost dejected by the whole thing. Shouldn't you be glowing with happiness?"

I stare out the window, not seeing anything because I'm too lost in my feelings. "It's not like I thought it would be," I whisper.

It was never supposed to be fake. Or feel like someone was whittling my heart like a piece of wood, slowly and painfully.

"How did you think it would be?" she asks.

"Oh, I don't know, glowing happiness, I guess?" I say, offering her a small smile and stealing her words. Truthfully, I thought it would feel like finally putting two perfect puzzle pieces together. It would be effortless.

It would be real.

But I know what I got myself into, and I agreed to this short-term torture for long-term gain. At the end of this, I can cut all ties, allow myself to grieve what will never be, and then move on and hopefully find someone who will love me as much as I deserve to be loved.

"You're not telling me something."

"I'm still processing it all. I'll fill you in on all the dirty details at some point."

She frowns, and I realize I'm not selling this at all. I need to pull on my big girl panties and make this seem real. I need to act like I would if Dom and I were really a couple.

"You know you can trust me, right?" she asks.

I smile, for real this time. "I know. Just give me some time to wrap my head around everything, okay?"

She nods and stands. "I'm here whenever you need me."

Before she gets to the door I stop her. "Hey Tess?" She spins around to face me and I continue, "I'm sorry things didn't work out with Ben. He was a great guy."

She smiles. "It's okay. I kinda figured you weren't quite ready yet like you said you were, which is perfect because Ben's still in love with his ex, so he's not really ready either. You both were exactly what the other person needed right then."

Then she turns around and continues heading for the door. As she exits, my assistant, Cooper, stands right outside the door holding a bouquet of gorgeous gardenias.

"These arrived for you. There's a card tucked in there too," he says.

Tessa smiles. "Oh, I think I know exactly who these are from."

I shoot her a look. "Mind your business," I say with a smile before grabbing the bouquet from Cooper and retreating into my office.

The card is a thick, smooth, cream cardstock, and I half expect there to be printed words on the card—since the bouquet was likely Shawna's idea—but I'm surprised when I see Dom's handwriting, a blocky scrawl I'd recognize anywhere.

Thinking about you. Dinner tonight?

I drop to my seat, the card firmly gripped in my fingers and my eyes rereading the words over and over again. I hate the part of me that gets giddy at the idea of Dom going into a flower shop and writing on this little card that he's thinking of me. That part of me wants this to be real and needs to get a grip on reality. Especially since Dom has never bought a girl flowers in his life.

Unfortunately, this gesture screams Shawna. But I agreed to play along and that's what I'm going to do.

Pulling my phone out of my desk drawer, I bring up my messages and find our last exchange. My heart pangs a little as I reread a few of our texts. Even now knowing the end of our friendship is looming, there's an ease to our conversation. But I suppose it's always been that way with us. Text messages and quiet conversations in the dark of night have always been where we seem to open up to each other the best.

If only I'd been brave enough years ago to confess my true feelings, maybe I wouldn't be in this situation. Maybe I'd already have moved on. But I suppose there's no point in wondering what if. He knows where I stand now and he doesn't feel the same. This version of Dom I'm experiencing is a lie.

I quickly tap out a text confirming our plans for tonight. Date number two. I don't know how many dates we'll end up going on in this charade, but I hope I can survive them all.

FOURTEEN

Dominic

"You wanted to see me, Coach?" I ask as I pop my head into Coach Fairbright's office. She's the first female defensive coach in Wolves history, and I have a lot of respect for her, but I suspect this is not a visit to pat me on the back for my hard work at practice today.

"Hey Dom, take a seat." She gestures to the chair across from her. Her tablet is in front of her, but she clicks it off and shoves it to the side. She leans forward, her elbows resting on the edge of her desk, and she folds her hands in front of her face. She wears her long dark hair in a no-nonsense ponytail, her bangs straight. Her hazel eyes don't give away any emotions to tell me what exactly to expect from this unplanned meeting.

"What's up?" I ask.

"A couple of things. First, are you okay?"

"Uh, yeah?"

She elaborates. "I mean with all the media stuff going on and the whole thing with Jen Summers. Are you doing okay?"

My shoulders sag. "Yeah, Coach. I'm alright."

She nods like that's exactly what she expected me to say even if we both know that's not the complete truth.

"Alright, then on to the next thing. You're one of my key players, Dom. You know I respect the hard work you put in on the field."

She holds up a finger to stop me when I open my mouth to respond. "But," she continues, "we both know playing for the pros is about more than just what you do on the field. You're judged just as harshly for what happens off it, and I gotta be honest, you're not doing yourself any favors with your recent behavior. Do you know how many conversations I've had with Denton and how many times I've had to convince him not to bench you?"

Coach Denton—our head coach—hasn't been happy with me for a while, but I didn't realize it had gotten so bad that Fairbright had to defend me.

Fuck.

She picks up her tablet and clicks it on before spinning it to show me what's on the screen. It's the article with the picture of Alayna and me at dinner the other night.

"I don't know what's going on with this, but don't drag that girl down with you, Dom. You either turn it all the way around or stop whatever game this is."

I meet her fierce and protective gaze. My heart pounds and there's a surge of pride through my body at how Alayna has managed to make everyone on this team fall in love with her and, more importantly, want to protect her.

Even if it's from me.

But it's not necessary. I'm fully aware of the mistakes I've made and how badly I've fucked up. I won't do it again, and definitely not to Laney.

"You don't have to worry, Coach." I glance back down at the tablet, my finger grazing over Alayna's form on the screen.

"Is it real, Dom?"

I meet her gaze and say something I'm only starting to realize has always been true. "It's always been real with her."

She nods slowly. "Then don't break her heart, okay? I'd hate to see what that would do to both of you, especially when I need you to be at your absolute best so Denton doesn't trade you."

"You got it, Coach."

It's an easy promise to make. I can only hope that at the end of all this, it's my heart that isn't broken.

"You're sure this is the right place?" Laney asks with a skeptical arch to her brow.

I glance down at my phone with the address for tonight's date that Shawna set up. She gave us minimal information—the time to arrive and what to wear—but never in a million years did I expect us to show up to a boutique opening that has a variety of celebs walking the small red carpet leading up to the front door and a swarm of paparazzi snapping pics.

Laney's eyes go wide. "Holy shit, is that a Kardashian?"

"Apparently this is the place to be."

She spins in her seat so she's facing me. "Dom, it's a clothing store."

I huff out a laugh because she's not wrong. "The address Shawna gave me matches. I'm assuming she wanted us to be seen with other folks."

I honestly have no idea what Shawna was thinking because this doesn't seem to be something that my image would benefit from, and it sure as hell isn't Laney's scene. I get out of the car that Shawna hired to take us and walk around to let Laney out.

"Dom! Dom, over here!" Flashes blind me as the press calls out my name, and it only gets worse once Laney's on my arm. "How does Jen feel about you moving on so quickly?"

I've never resented someone the way I resent Jen Summers right now—and myself for even considering hooking up with someone whose entire life is in the spotlight. I was well-known before, but our scandal has thrust me into a whole new level of stardom that I honestly would rather do without.

Laney's fingers grip my suit coat tightly, and her head is ducked to avoid the lights. My stomach sours at the whole dog and pony show that we have to put on. This isn't what I had in mind when I thought we'd have to fake date for the press. I thought I'd get more time with my best friend, more time to dive deeper into these newly emerged feelings.

Instead, we're both forced to go to some fancy opening for a boutique that doesn't appear to be either of our styles.

We get through the frenzy of press and emerge into a clean space with high-end fashion designs.

"I feel like I'm in that scene from *Pretty Woman*," Laney whispers, and I can't fight back my smile as I look down at her.

She put her blonde hair in this fancy updo that exposes her neck, and it's taking everything in me not to nuzzle that spot just behind her ear and kiss my way down her throat. I look away quickly and curse the fact that we're in public and there's no easy or discreet way to adjust the situation happening in my pants.

"Dom!" This time it's a voice I recognize calling out to me. I turn my head to see Mikey Paxton, a retired linebacker for the Wolves and one of the nicest guys I've ever met.

He saunters over to us, his signature smile on his face.

"Mikey, man, how the hell have you been?"

His smile grows. "Never better, man."

Before he can continue, a pixie of a woman slides her hand over Mikey's arm as she snuggles close. She's half his size, but the way he looks at her with stars in his eyes tells me she's the one in charge in their relationship.

"Mikey, you gonna introduce me to your friends?"

"Dom, Dom's lady, this is my wife and the genius behind this fine establishment, Sapphire Rain."

She smiles at me and then Laney. "You can call me Saf. And I'm sure you don't go by 'Dom's lady,'" she says to Laney.

"Alayna."

"So nice to meet you—both of you. And thank you for coming to my opening."

"Uh, sure, anytime," I say, even though this is still the last place I'd want to be. But I get why Shawna chose it now that I'm seeing the connection to a fellow Wolves player. As the night goes on, more athletes arrive, as well as other celebrities—some pretty big ones and some lesser known. It's a melting pot of fame, and it's clear Sapphire's got some star power backing her business.

But all night long, there's a distance between Laney and me, one I know won't go away if these are the kinds of dates we're supposed to be going on for the next six months. If I'm going to use this time to my advantage, I need dates that will allow me to remind Laney how good we are together, not further drive us apart by making her feel like she doesn't belong in my world.

Because that couldn't be further from the truth.

She *is* my whole world.

FIFTEEN

Alayna

This is our second red carpet event in as many days. Apparently Shawna got us on the list for this hot new premiere that she couldn't pass up. There was also a conversation about how it's better for us to be hot and heavy quickly and then we can spread our dates out the longer this ruse goes on.

I'll be honest, I'm way more excited about this movie premiere than I was about the boutique opening—even if Saf and Mikey were the cutest odd couple I've ever met.

One thing I'm not excited about is the flashing lights of the press that are everywhere—the select few on the red carpet, the many that are taking pictures behind partitions set up, and the ones that line the hallways and try to catch anyone who they think could give them a juicy tidbit. I don't know how Dom can deal with all this chaos after games, even if it's not nearly to the level that we've been exposed to over the past two dates.

My palms are sweaty, but I'm afraid to wipe them on my dress. I'm sure the press would have a field day with that, and I'm more aware than ever that this is Jen

Summers's territory. I've seen her walk with the grace of a swan when she's on the red carpet. The media loves her, and I have no doubt I'm going to hear her name all night long as people question Dom about his new "relationship" with a nobody.

Speak of the devil, a large hand wraps around mine and squeezes twice. His warm breath brushes against my ear, and I barely restrain the shiver it provokes.

"Breathe, Sunshine. Don't give them any more power than they deserve. They're nothing special, and it doesn't matter what they think of you."

"Of course it matters," I mutter under my breath so no one else can hear. Then I turn to whisper in his ear, but he hasn't moved back and our lips are only a whisper away from each other. My gaze shoots to his, and I must be imagining it, but it almost looks like his blue eyes darken slightly at our proximity. His gaze is locked on mine and I hold my breath. I couldn't break away from this stare-off if I wanted to. My chest tightens, and any nerves I had are quickly replaced by a fierce desire that makes my clit tingle between my legs and my stomach clench with want. My body leans closer to him without my permission, but the wild thing is his seems to do the same.

"Laney," he whispers, saying my name like it's a prayer and a plea all at once. No man has ever said my name that way.

"Dom?" It's a question because I don't understand what's going on between us. He's not brought up the feelings I confessed since we agreed to this fake dating arrangement. Is this just for the cameras or is this real?

I'm not sure my heart can take it if this is what he looks like when he's faking because it's the realest moment I've ever had.

"Dom! Dom! Why aren't you here with Jen Summers?" a voice calls out, and it's like being doused with a bucket of ice.

I break eye contact and take a step away, but Dom's hand is still holding mine, and his grip tightens at my retreat. His Adam's apple bobs as he swallows thickly and stares at me for a moment longer before he turns toward the voice that called out and pastes on a smile.

My throat tightens as my stomach rolls because his expression is so clear—at least to me—that he's faking the smile with the reporter.

Does that mean he wasn't faking it with me? But that can't be right because he looked at me like...I can't even go there. I shake away the thoughts and follow his lead, pasting my own fake smile on and preparing myself for the barrage of questions about why it's me on his arm instead of Jen Summers.

I'm so sick of hearing her name and being compared to her.

The questions thrown at us are as asinine as I expected, but there's a silver lining when I catch a glance of Heath Monroe, the lead actor in the movie and a man that I've always found insanely attractive. His smile makes women's panties damp the world over.

I squeeze Dom's hand and when he catches who I'm fangirling over, he doesn't bother to hide his eye roll. "Are you seriously still obsessed with that guy?"

"Are you kidding me? Of course I am. Not only is he gorgeous, but he also visits sick kids at the children's hospital every month when he's not away filming, and he's so incredible in his movies—"

"Okay, okay, I get it. You worship the ground he walks on."

I arch a brow. "Someone sounds a little salty."

He lets go of my hand and slides his warm palm along my lower back before pulling my body flush with his.

His voice drops to a low grumble that's sexier than it should be. "Maybe I just wish you'd fangirl over me like that."

It's hard to find my voice because he's looking at me like he did earlier, and it scrambles all the thoughts from my head.

"Maybe you should be as amazing as he is," I whisper.

He narrows his eyes and I see the unspoken words. *Challenge accepted.*

"Let's go meet him," he says, already sweeping me along with him as he makes his way toward Heath Monroe.

"What!" I squeak. I can't meet Heath Monroe. What would I even say? Oh my God, he's right there.

I swoon a little as he smiles at the camera, and then Dom calls his name as if they're buddies even though I know they're not—I'd kill Dom if he kept that kind of secret from me when he knows how much I love Heath.

"Heath, I'm Dom Smith, and this is my friend Alayna Pritchard. She's a big fan." I'm sure no one else notices, but I know him well enough to practically hear the eye roll as he says it.

Heath turns the full weight of his stare to me, and I nearly collapse under the heaviness of his green-eyed gaze. "I-I'm a huge f-fan."

Oh my God, Laney, pull yourself together.

I clear my throat and try again. "I loved you in *A Winter's War*. The way you portrayed that character was incredible."

His smile grows and then he nods. "I know, honey. That's why I won an Oscar for it. Do you want an autograph or something? I need to keep moving, so the cameras get me while my makeup is pristine."

My smile falters for a moment. "Oh, um, right. Would you be willing to take a picture?"

"Sure thing, honey. Come on over here." He spreads his arm wide to make room for me to snuggle against his side, but I hesitate because he's giving off smarmy vibes that I did not expect from Heath Monroe.

Brushing it off as just a by-product of being off-kilter from the intensity between Dom and me, I move to stand next to him, and he immediately slides his arm down my back until it rests high on my ass.

My smile freezes completely and my cheeks heat with embarrassment. What the hell is happening? Dom's gaze narrows and he arches one brow in question, but I shake it off and push my shoulders back, trying not to be so stiff.

Then Heath has to go and open his mouth and shatter whatever illusions I had that he was a good guy. "Ditch your football fool and meet me in my hotel room," he whispers in my ear, prattling off the hotel he's apparently staying at—which seems weird since he lives in Los Angeles—and his room number.

"All good?" he asks Dom as I remain frozen and speechless next to him.

Dom nods but his concerned gaze never leaves mine.

And then as if he needed to add a cherry on top, Heath Monroe smacks my ass and walks away as if nothing happened.

Dom glowers, and his fists clench at his side as he moves toward me. "Did he just do what I think he did?" he asks, his voice low and threatening.

Oh shit, I know that tone. That's his I'm-going-to-lay-some-asshole-out voice.

Time to go.

Forget the premiere. I'm not feeling it anymore anyway. It takes some convincing, but eventually Dom acquiesces, and we ditch the premiere before the movie ever starts. We were seen and photographed which is really all Shawna wanted anyway, I'm sure.

And I learned another valuable lesson. Never meet your heroes.

Dominic

I've got a reality TV star at the table to my left and a Hollywood A-lister at the table to my right. Alayna sits across from me, staring resolutely at the menu while camera lights flash from outside. I have no idea if they're taking pictures of us or the celebrities on either side of me, but I'm starting to resent Shawna's choice in restaurant. I might've been a party boy, but this restaurant is way too flashy for even me. I need to have a conversation with her and Trey about how much input she'll have in our dates, because this is the third one that's been a bust, and I'm losing my patience.

What's worse is I know how uncomfortable Alayna is with all the attention, even if she's playing it off like a champ. She hasn't said anything about the flowers I sent her before our first date, or the bouquet I sent after that creep Heath Monroe ruined the movie premiere for her. I've never sent a girl flowers in my life, but I know I need to step out of my comfort zone for her. I have a lot of work to do to prove how much she means to me.

"What are you going to order?"

She doesn't look up from the menu as she says, "Hmm... the salmon sounds pretty good, so I might have that."

I fight a shudder. "I don't know how you can eat that. Fish is gross."

She rolls her pretty eyes, but her lips tilt up in a smile, and I can't stop my own from spreading. "I don't understand why you're such a fish hater. It's delicious."

She finally looks at me and lets out a laugh at the pure mortification on my face. The sound sends warmth through my belly and my smile grows. "You're crazy."

"Nice comeback, Ace," she teases, using the nickname she graced me with in high school. It's been weeks since I've heard it, and I didn't realize how much I missed it until this moment.

The waiter comes over and takes our orders before leaving us alone. Well, as alone as you can be in a restaurant that feels like it's explicitly set up for celebrities to be visible to the paparazzi. There are restaurants that cater to celebs who want privacy, and then there are restaurants like this one that cater to those who want to be talked about in the media and entertainment outlets. I've never purposely put myself in the limelight like this, and I have to admit it's disconcerting.

A quick glance at the couple next to us only enhances that feeling. The couple are arguing with smiles pasted on their faces so anyone taking pictures would have no idea. The Hollywood A-lister on my other side is laughing at a joke that's not funny, and I'm guessing it's some producer or director sitting across from her that she's trying to schmooze. Her acting skills are far superior to the reality TV star's, that's for sure, but the whole situation just reeks of *fake*.

When I look back at Alayna, she's already watching me,

a thoughtful expression on her face. "What are you think-ing?" she asks.

Leaning forward, I lower my voice so no one at the nearby tables can hear us. "I'm thinking I miss going through the In-N-Out drive-thru and then taking our food to the beach and eating it with sand between our toes."

She smiles, but it doesn't quite reach her eyes before she drops her gaze to the table. "We've come a long way since those early days in California."

"Maybe. But this place still isn't us."

She shrugs and looks around before staring at me point-blank. "I don't know. It could be."

I part my lips to argue, but our waiter shows up with our dinner and places two large white plates in front of us. On mine sits a brown piece of meat that's half the size of my wallet and decorated with frilly garnishes that don't look edible. Alayna's plate doesn't look much better. She has a piece of salmon the size of her pointer finger.

The waiter smiles at us. "Enjoy."

Before he steps away, I say, "Um...sorry, but where's the rest of our meal?"

"Excuse me?" he replies, his smile stiffening.

"Dom," Laney says, but I don't look at her before I continue.

"The rest of our meal. This is..." I glance at the plate, trying to find the words for what this is. "Well, it looks more like an appetizer, honestly."

The waiter's smile evaporates. "This is exactly what you ordered." Then he walks away.

I stare after him for a moment before I turn back around and find Laney laughing into her hand.

Her laughter is contagious and soon my own escapes. "This is the most pathetic-looking meal I've ever seen."

She nods and then snorts, causing us both to burst into an even bigger fit of laughter. We're getting looks from the tables next to us, and the cameras out the windows are flashing like crazy, but neither of us care.

"I'm afraid if I sneeze, my food might blow away," Laney chokes out, causing both of us to keel over in a new fit of laughter.

"What's the macro numbers for flavored foam?" I ask.

Tears form in the corner of Laney's eyes as she braces herself against the table, her whole chest heaving with laughter. My own laughter starts to subside, but I can't stop smiling to save my life.

I love her like this—uninhibited, beautiful, and most of all, happy.

Throwing my napkin on the table, I stand up and drop a hundred on the table before offering a hand to Laney. "Alright, enough of this nonsense. Let's get some real food."

With her eyes still bright with laughter, she doesn't hesitate to place her hand in mine. "You're on, Smith."

I pull her up from her seat and keep her hand in mine as I move swiftly out of the restaurant.

It takes us thirty minutes to drive to her favorite taco truck and order—fish tacos for her and a chicken burrito for me. We eat at a picnic table nearby, surrounded by a handful of strangers as we chow on some of the best Mexican food I've eaten in my life—apart from Gabe's mom's tamales.

It's the best date I've ever been on. Hands down.

But it's made even better by Laney's relaxed shoulders and genuine smile. Her eyes aren't tight at the corners anymore, and it feels like any other night we'd go out for dinner. It feels more like how I imagined this being. Not fake or forced, but real and relaxed.

It feels like *us*.

"Tell me something I don't know," I say before taking the last bite of my burrito.

"That's a long list," she says, but her voice is light and teasing so I don't take it personally. She dramatically taps her chin while she hums.

"Hmm, something you don't know. About me? Or about anything?"

"About you obviously."

She shrugs. "You know all there is to know about me," she says and then takes a bite of her taco.

I fold my hands together and lean forward on the table. "I doubt that's true. I've been an especially shitty friend lately, so I'm sure there's something that's happened in the last few months you probably didn't tell me. Come on, lay it on me."

Her mouth turns down as her eyes drop to the table for a second, but I already saw the sadness that glimmered in those blue depths. Her voice is soft, almost apologetic when she says, "Here's the thing, Dom. I did tell you everything, even when you were spectacularly shitty, so if there's something you don't know then it's probably because you weren't listening to me. And I'm not really sure what to tell you now because I don't know what you were paying attention to and what you weren't."

A sharp pain slices through me as her words make their mark. "I'm sorry," I say, my voice hoarse. I know she didn't say it to be hurtful—the soft, apologetic tone made that clear —but her honesty hurts, even if I know I need to hear it. I'd rather she be painfully honest with me than keep her guard up like she's been doing lately.

"I believe you." Her eyes warn me that the next words out of her mouth are also going to hurt—the apology in them still crystal clear, but the resolute strength there too. "But I don't know if 'I'm sorry' is good enough anymore."

Silence sits heavy between us as I process her words. I know what I need to do. I just don't know if anything will be enough to save us. And that guts me in a way nothing has since my mom died—that same hollow emptiness spreading inside me.

"Will you come somewhere with me?"

She nibbles her lip for a split second, then says, "Where?"

"Do you trust me?"

"Yes," she says, not hesitating this time. It's something, and I'll take anything I can get from her at this point.

"Then let's go." I stand up and reach out my hand for her. We're still supposed to be on our date, but I also like the feel of her soft palm wrapped in mine.

When she takes my hand, a mix of calmness and relief fills me. I'll do whatever it takes to keep this woman in my life, even if I know I don't deserve her.

SEVENTEEN

Alayna

We end up at the beach, but not just any beach. *Our* beach. The first beach we drove to when we both moved to LA. The second we hit the sand, I slide out of my shoes—a cute pair of wedges—and carry them by two fingers in the heels. Dom walks beside me with a spare blanket he had in his trunk in one arm and his other hand holding mine.

He's been doing that a lot tonight, and it's kind of messing with my head—maybe because I'm still confused about those "moments" we kept having at the movie premiere.

We've never shied away from physical touch, but they were hugs mostly, maybe the occasional cuddle on the nights we'd fall asleep at each other's place. But we never held hands for extended lengths of time.

I don't know what to do with this version of Dom. And I hate him a little bit for making me fall a little more for him when I'm trying so hard to fall *less*.

The wind picks up and I shiver, moving closer to Dom's warmth. He loosens his grip on my hand, and for a second, my heart falters thinking he's going to pull away, but then he wraps his arm around my shoulders, pulling me tighter against him.

I'm so tired of fighting my feelings for him, so I don't do the smart thing and pull away like I know I should. Instead, I lean into him, soaking up his body heat and feeling his firm muscles underneath his clothes that are a reminder of how strong he is, even in moments when he's a gentle giant like right now.

"Maybe the beach in January was a bad idea..."

I can't stop the giggle that escapes. We both grew up in Idaho and can handle some cold-ass winters—much colder than anything we get in Southern California—and he knows it.

We find a spot about halfway down the beach, and Dom spreads out the blanket before we settle down on it side by side, our shoulders and hips touching and his warmth offering me comfort.

The only sound for a long time is the crashing of the waves hitting the shore. Peace settles deep in my bones, my toes in the sand grounding me.

How many nights have we spent just like this in the past? And how many times did I wish for the courage to finally tell him how I felt? I thought maybe coming here under the pretense of being a couple might ruin my happy place, but instead, it settles me, makes me feel safe from the inevitable pain that will come when this all ends.

"Tell me something I don't know," I whisper, afraid to break the silence but needing desperately to get out of my own head.

I can feel the weight of his stare against my cheek and can only ignore it so long before I meet his gaze.

"My dad keeps calling me," he says softly like he's confessing it.

"Have you answered any of them?"

"No." He focuses back on the ocean, vast and endless, and not for the first time, I wish I could read his mind.

"Why not?"

He shrugs, but there's something about the stiffness in his shoulders that makes me think he's holding back. "Nothing to say."

"Be honest."

He turns his head, his crystal-blue eyes filled with emotions that he's only ever let me see. "What do you want me to say, Laney? That I can't stand to hear his voice? Even after he told me he's dying, I still can't find it in me to forgive him for what he did." He looks back at the ocean, but I don't think he's really seeing it. "I feel like a bad son. And yet at the same time, our relationship has been strained for so long...I don't know if there's anything left to salvage, or anything to feel bad about."

"How much longer does he have?"

He drops his head, looking at the sand between his bent legs. His elbows drape casually over his knees, but his shoulders sag as he whispers, "I don't know. I haven't asked him for details."

I reach out and rub his back because I can't *not* touch him when I know he's hurting. Despite what he says, I know Dom will mourn his dad's death. He'll mourn the relationship they lost all those years ago after his mom died. He'll mourn the memories that were never created because his dad turned out to be someone different than he'd grown up thinking he was.

His voice is broken when he speaks after several minutes of only the sound of the waves crashing. "I can't lose you too."

I almost don't hear him over the roar of the ocean, but when the words finally hit me, they hit me hard.

I wish I could tell him he'll never lose me. The truth is I don't want to lose Dom. He's been such an essential part of me for so long, I don't really know who I am without him. But I don't know how to keep him and not feel constantly brokenhearted because he doesn't reciprocate my feelings. It's an awful pickle to be in because either way I lose. I can't reassure him like he wants. Not now. Not with our relationship teetering on the edge of collapse.

Not when he doesn't love me the way I love him.

Instead of saying anything, I lean my head on his shoulder. Barely a moment passes before he rests his head on mine and we both stare out at the ocean.

I'm not sure how long we sit there together, not saying a thing, when his phone dings. He pulls it out, and the screen illuminates the darkness surrounding us. On it is a text from Shawna with a link and the words "Great job, you two!"

My stomach sinks with dread as he clicks the link, and an article pops up with the two of us at the restaurant earlier tonight. We're both laughing which means it must've been when we were making fun of the ridiculous portion sizes. The headline catches my eye next. *Jen Summers long forgotten as notorious party boy Dominic Smith dines with new lady love.*

It speculates on our relationship and lists my name. It's the first time in all these years that I've been linked to Dom like this since he was always careful to keep me out of the spotlight before, and it's a little jarring to see my name plastered in the media.

"Well, I guess there's no turning back now," I say.

He glances down at me. "Do you regret agreeing to do this?"

I meet his gaze, and my heart starts to pound a little harder at the intensity in his eyes and how close our faces are. "Not yet," I whisper.

But I have no doubt I will soon.

Shawna is pushing for us to level up our PDA, but the thought of my first kiss with Dom happening in front of cameras guts me.

I've imagined him kissing me dozens of times, but never with an audience. It was always private. Always something that was just ours.

"What are you thinking?" he whispers, and his breath brushes across my face, igniting an inferno that pulses between my thighs. Why does he have to be so attractive? These small moments where he's so attentive to me have always been my kryptonite.

But then he does something he's never done before. His gaze drops down to my lips, and again, I swear his eyes get darker before his intense stare connects with mine.

I can't lie to him when he looks at me like this. "I don't want our first kiss to be in front of cameras," I whisper.

Now I'm positive his eyes flare before he lowers his head until he's only a breath away from me. "Tell me to stop if you don't want this," he says, his voice hoarse and lower than I've ever heard it.

I stay silent, and that silence is rewarded when his firm lips finally press against mine.

The kiss is soft, almost tentative at first before he lets out a low, deep sound that vibrates through his lips into the kiss and then he surges forward. One hand wraps around the back of my neck, holding me to him, while the other wraps around my waist, securing me against him as he devours my mouth like no man ever has. My pulse races, and my body thrums with a need so intense my whole body feels like it's on the edge of a steep cliff, teetering into the abyss.

His tongue slides against my lips and I part them instantly. Our tongues glide against each other like we've kissed a million times instead of only once.

This.

This was how I always imagined it. Just the two of us sitting in front of an endless ocean getting lost in each other.

And I hate that it's as perfect as anything I ever imagined.

EIGHTEEN

Dominic

Fuck.

I stare at the latest article link Shawna just sent over, and my stomach tightens into a knot. I didn't think we'd been followed after we left the restaurant, but there's a picture of us taken at the beach. They had to be far away, but with a long enough lens to get the perfect close-up of our kiss.

The best fucking kiss of my damn life. The kiss that's had my head in a spiral ever since we stopped. Why did I wait so long to kiss her? Why haven't we been kissing this whole time? Why have I been wasting my time with other women when the perfect one was right in front of me all along?

The only answer I've managed to come up with is that I'm a total and complete idiot, which is news to no one at this point, but shit. I can't believe I've wasted so much time.

But then again, everything that happened with my dad and his affair fucked with my head, and I doubt I would've been a good boyfriend to her if this had happened sooner. We might not even be friends now if it had.

That knot in my stomach tightens.

I look back down at my phone and rub my hand over the back of my neck. I know I need to call Laney and tell her, but she'll think it was all set up. Most of all, I'm worried she'll think I was in on it, and I don't want her to regret any part of that kiss.

I sure as hell don't.

If anything, I'm now counting down the seconds until I can kiss her again.

My phone dings with another text from Shawna. Another media outlet got a copy of the photo, and I know it's only a matter of time before Alayna finds out about it on her own. I need her to hear it from me, so I call her, even if everything in me is screaming to drive over to her place so I can see her face.

She answers after the third ring. "Hello?" Her voice is groggy like she just woke up, and I'd give just about anything to be next to her right now.

"Hey. Sorry, did I wake you?"

"Yeah, but it's okay. I need to get up anyway. What's up?"

I push through the growing dread in my gut. "I wanted you to hear it from me before you saw it for yourself, but we made headlines from our date yesterday."

"Okayyy. Wasn't that the point of that overpriced restaurant?"

I close my eyes. "The picture wasn't from the restaurant. It was from the beach."

There's a beat of weighted silence before she says, "Oh."

I can't pick up on her tone with only one word, so I fill the continuing silence. "I had no idea. I thought we lost them before we even got to the taco truck. I didn't realize they followed us to the beach." She doesn't say anything. "Laney? You know I didn't plan this, right?"

"Yeah," she says, but her voice lacks conviction.

"Laney, that kiss—"

"We don't have to talk about it, Dom. I appreciate you trying to make it happen when the press weren't around so I would be comfortable. Honestly, this probably sells our story better, don't you think? People are more likely to believe it's real now."

Whatever words I was ready to speak die a quick death on my tongue. That dread that was building in my gut turns sour, and there's a sharp ache in my chest at how nonchalant she suddenly sounds.

"Listen, thanks for telling me so I wasn't blindsided, but I need to get going. I'll see you at your game tomorrow. I'm flying out this afternoon."

She's flying to Philadelphia where they're holding the Super Bowl this year. Shawna suggested it, but Laney had already planned to attend. She'd never miss it, but now I wish she wasn't just coming as my friend.

That kiss last night changed things. Changed *me*. And I'm scared shitless what this means going forward.

The crowd is going wild, but all I can hear is the sound of my harsh breath as I get in position and focus on the next play. The score is 7-7 in the fourth quarter, and there's no way in hell I'm letting these guys get past me and score another touchdown.

Not today. Not for *this* game.

The Big Game.

The one all professional football players aspire to get to.

Today, the ultimate champions are going to be the Wolves. I don't care what the scoreboard says right now. I know our offense can get it done, but it's time for the Fierce Four to shut down the opposing offense so they can get that chance.

Gabe shoots me a look before I slide my gaze over to Romel and Tyler, the other members of the Fierce Four. Combined, we're a powerhouse like the NFL hasn't seen in years.

The ball snaps, and every player breaks into motion. This is the only kind of chaos I love. Where everyone is scrambling and running to get where they need to go. Adrenaline spikes through my bloodstream and brings with it a strange, buzzing sort of calm. My gaze focuses on my target, trusting my teammates to do their job and close any gaps.

The receiver I'm watching darts toward me before changing course and heading toward the middle. Ty sees him and rushes forward to stop his progress. He tackles the player, ending the opposing team's play on the fourth down. Ty jumps back up, and the rest of the Fierce Four rush at him, slapping his back and cheering him on.

That's how we do this.

We rush off to the sidelines as our offense runs onto the field. A glance at the clock tells me this is our last chance. If they get that ball back again, they'll either win or force us into overtime. We need to finish this now.

Jack calls the play and then gets in position. After the snap, he steps back, bouncing back and forth, his gaze focused on two options—Will Edmonson or Matt Fischer. Will gets open and Jack lets the ball loose. It spirals through the air, and we hold our breath as it soars straight to its intended target. Will catches the ball, spins, dodging a tackle, and then bursts forth racing toward the end zone.

Our entire sideline is standing, jumping, yelling for him to keep going. He's thirty yards away, then twenty, then ten. The opposing defense finally catches up to him and he jumps, extending his arms straight out as the defense takes him down to the ground. We stand with bated breath, waiting for the ref's call.

I swear time slows until the ref shoots his hands straight up into the air.

Touchdown!

"Let's fucking go!" I shout as we all lose our shit on the sidelines, hugging each other and smiling wide.

Our kicker finishes it off, giving us the extra point, and now we're ahead by seven. There's two minutes left on the clock, which isn't much time, but it's possible they could throw a Hail Mary and catch up with us. We just need to hold them off.

Our defense runs back out onto the field, ready to secure our impending win with our lives. There's no way we're letting them through us now. Not when we're so close to victory, we can taste it.

These two minutes are the longest of my life, but we successfully hold them off, and when that clock hits zero, silver confetti falls onto the field, and the rest of the team rushes out onto the green turf. All of us hug each other, screaming our heads off. There's always a crazy rush of adrenaline after a win, but this is some next-level shit.

I hug each of my best friends, Gabe, Romel, and Ty, and then I go on the hunt for the only other person I want to see after such a huge win. My gaze scans the faces of the growing crowd surrounding us. I see Danae, Gabe's woman, jump into his arms and kiss him hard.

An ache grows in my chest, followed by an unfamiliar desperation.

I need to find my girl.

Frantically searching the crowd now, I search every face for the one I want to see most. I know she's here; she texted me before the game.

A hand wraps around my arm and tugs me back. I spin, about to brush off the person when my gaze connects with the familiar deep-blue of Laney's eyes.

She's smiling up at me with such pure joy and excitement—no sign of any of the tension that's been present since my scandal. This is the woman who has always supported me, always shown up as my biggest cheerleader, whether it was a college game or a professional one. She's always been there.

And how have I treated her for her loyalty?

A rock tumbles in my gut, but I brush it away. It's not too late for me to do better. For me to prove to her that I won't take her for granted ever again.

That I'm no longer the blind idiot I've been for the last decade.

I pull her into my arms, hugging her tight against my sweaty body, and instead of being grossed out like women of my past, she hugs me tighter and laughs loudly in my ear.

"I'm so proud of you, Dom."

She pulls back slightly and our gazes connect. That tightness in my chest that's been growing whenever she's near seems to get even worse. I glance down at her lips and fight against the longing to lean down and kiss her.

But I can't quite fight my body's response, and I lean my head down to rest on hers. "Thanks for being here."

"There's nowhere else I'd be."

We stare at each other, the air buzzing with the growing tension between us. Someone jostles behind me pushing me forward, and I hold Laney close to my body so she doesn't lose her own footing. Her arms tighten around me and her breath quickens.

"Laney..." I choke out her name, part plea, part desire.

Her gaze drops to my lips and then her tongue darts out to lick along her bottom lip. I'm not even sure she's aware of it, but it breaks whatever resolve I had, and I lean down and brush my lips against hers. She melts against my body, and despite the deafening sound around us, it almost feels like we're alone. I close my eyes, savoring the taste of her, the feel of her plush lips against mine, the way her tongue darts out hesitantly to lick against my lips—like she's afraid I'll deny her.

I couldn't deny her if my life depended on it.

I've never wanted a woman's kiss as badly as I want this one.

I can't hear her whimper, but I feel the vibration of it where our lips meet, and that only encourages me to kiss her deeper.

Someone bumps into me again, and I reluctantly pull away from her. I can tell in my periphery that the field is full of bodies and people celebrating, but I can't look away from the woman in front of me.

How can I prove to her that she means the world to me?

And not just as my best friend...

NINETEEN

Alayna

My lips still tingle as we move off the field. The players head to the locker room to clean up before we'll all head over to a banquet hall to celebrate more. I join the other wives and girlfriends, or WAGs as they're often referred to, my mind buzzing from that brain-melting kiss.

I know there are a ton of cameras around, but I wasn't expecting him to kiss me like that. I expected a peck on the lips, but clearly Dom didn't want any doubts in the minds of the press. Instead, he's only planted doubts in my own head.

I don't know if I'm strong enough to fake this if he's going to kiss me like that. I'm having a very hard time remembering that it's not real. And that's dangerous—for my heart and my sanity.

Danae comes up to me, practically glowing with happiness, and reaches her arms out for a hug. "They did it! I'm so excited."

I laugh lightly. Two months ago, she didn't know a single thing about football, and now she's a huge fan and the biggest supporter for Gabe. It's nice seeing them so happy.

He deserves the love of a good woman like Danae, and I have no doubt these two will go the distance.

"Hey, you okay?" she asks, a slight frown marring her face.

"Yeah, I'm good. Still reeling." I paste on a smile, hoping it looks more authentic than it feels.

She arches her eyebrow, and her lips tilt up in a smirk. "You mean from that kiss?" She fans her face and then leans forward. "I told Gabe there was something going on between you and Dom, but he didn't believe me. Not until we saw that picture of you two kissing at the beach."

It gets harder to hold my smile at her mention of our first kiss—the one that was supposed to be just for us, but instead has become part of this whole farce. But Dom's career is relying on my ability to sell this as real, so I don't deny her statement.

"Yeah, I guess it just took us a while to figure out what was between us."

She smiles at me, and it's a smile that happy, in-love people always seem to have whenever they talk to other happy, in-love people. It's a knowing smile. I just wish I understood what I'm supposed to know because right now all I know is this whole thing has become even more emotionally confusing than I thought it would be.

And that's saying something.

Fortunately, I'm saved from having to talk about my relationship with Dom by the other WAGs coming over. Paige, Jack's wife, cradles her small baby bump which seemed to appear out of nowhere overnight. Gina, Will's fiancée, is next to her, a gorgeous smile on her face. Nikki, Matt's fiancée, and Emma, Luke Carter's fiancée, follow behind them.

I've befriended these ladies over the years, always grateful for how down-to-earth they've been and accepting of me even when I wasn't technically a wife or a girlfriend. It feels horrible to lie to them now, but it's even sadder to consider the idea of not having them in my life when Dom and I go our separate ways. Will they still want to be friends with me when I'm no longer part of the Wolves family? Will I have to say goodbye to everyone just so I can get over Dom?

This is the downside of falling for your best friend that no one talks about. When your lives have been as entwined as mine and Dom's for so long, you end up having a lot of the same friends. What happens when you have to cut ties to save yourself from endless heartache? Is this what divorced couples go through?

"Hey, you okay?" Danae whispers next to me, and I realize my smile has slipped thanks to the depressing direction of my thoughts.

"I'm fine," I say, trying to build up my walls so I can make it through tonight. I've never been a good liar, but I especially struggle to lie to my friends, and these ladies are some of my closest.

Her eyes narrow, and she dips her head so the other ladies won't overhear. "I call bullshit."

"I'll tell you later," I murmur in a lame attempt to buy myself some time. I signed an NDA, so I can't actually tell her anything, but obviously I'm not selling that I'm as happy and in love as I'm supposed to be.

Excitement fills the air as the other WAGs join us and we talk about how great the game was. We start snacking on the canapés and chatting until the guys finally join us. Dom wraps an arm around my waist, securing me to his side, and my belly lets loose a flurry of butterflies at the possessive touch. At the same time, my heart splinters with longing for it to be real.

A server walks by with a tray of champagne, and I grab two flutes and hand one to Dom, already bringing mine up to my lips, hoping the alcohol will steady my nerves. But instead of taking it from me, he waves it away.

He leans his head close, his breath brushing against my ear and sending a shiver of want down my spine. "I quit drinking."

I snap my gaze to meet his. "Since when?"

His crystal-blue eyes stare into mine as if he's trying to see into my soul. "Since the scandal. Most—okay, all—of my bad decisions came after alcohol. I don't want to be that guy anymore. I don't want to keep letting down the people who mean the most to me, so I decided the alcohol had to go. Maybe not forever, but for the foreseeable future."

"You didn't tell me."

He shrugs. "It didn't seem important compared to everything else."

He's wrong. It's very important. He's been a party boy almost as long as I've known him. It's a defining trait, so giving it up means he's one hundred percent serious about changing his life. It's not just a publicity stunt until things die down.

Somehow that realization leaves me reeling. If he's serious about this, then what else might he be serious about?

No. Don't go there.

Why do I always do this? Why do I always make excuses for trying to believe that I mean more to him than I actually do? I've got to stop. I've got to stop seeing potential that isn't there.

Dom might be sober now, but he's doing it for his career, nothing else. This team means the world to him, and he's made that clear more than once. He'd be completely gutted to be ripped away from the Fierce Four. Hell, what even is the Fierce Four if they don't have Dom?

"Are you upset I didn't tell you?" Dom asks, breaking through my thoughts.

"No. I guess not." It's the truth. I'm not upset, but I am confused. It's like trying to make sense of a puzzle when you don't have all the pieces. But I do have all the pieces—my heart and my head just aren't in agreement with the picture those pieces present when I put them together.

He drops a kiss to the top of my head and then turns to the group. I didn't notice the other guys had also joined us.

"It's about fucking time," Ty says, gesturing between Dom and me with his beer bottle that he must've gotten over at the bar on the other side of the room.

"What's that supposed to mean?" Dom asks, his arm tightening around my waist.

"It means I called it ages ago. I always knew you two would end up together. You were way too protective of her to be 'just a friend,'" he says using air quotes. There's something else in his smile and the way he looks between Dom and me.

Dom looks down at me, and I fight the urge to fidget and pull out of his arms. I hate this. I hate lying to our friends. But Dom doesn't seem bothered at all. If anything, he gets this soft expression in his eyes that I can't quite figure out and then turns back to Ty.

"Yeah, well, nobody said I was smart. Just took me a little longer than it should've to see what was right in front of me."

A sharp pain stabs my heart, and it takes everything I have not to drop my smile. I've imagined this scenario so many times—those exact words coming out of his mouth—

but I never imagined how painful it would feel. Sometimes the universe gives you exactly what you've asked for and not at all in the way you wanted it.

I should be more careful about how I phrase my intentions.

I put my champagne glass to my lips and take a large swallow of the bubbly liquid. It's not nearly strong enough to get me through this, but it'll have to do.

Everyone smiles at us like they expect Dom to get on one knee and propose any moment, given that this was apparently a long time coming. Through it all, I fight to keep my heartbreak hidden, knowing this is all temporary and in a few months these people might not even want to be my friends anymore. The stabbing ache in my heart gets worse, and all I can do is hope that when all's said and done, I'll go somewhere new and never have to feel this way again.

Even if I suspect that Dom's absence in my life will leave a hole too big to fill.

TWENTY

Dominic

It feels completely natural to hold Alayna close to me while I sip my water and chat with the guys. One of the Wolves reps comes over periodically to pull one of us away for quick interviews with the press, but overall, it's a great way to end an incredible night.

A waiter passes by, and Alayna swaps out her now empty champagne glass with a fresh one. I watch her take a large sip and then widen her smile as Paige talks to her about a girls' weekend trip they've been planning.

Alayna's never been a big drinker, so I know something's bothering her, and I'm determined to get to the bottom of it so she can enjoy tonight with me. I want her to feel as relaxed and happy as I do.

"Excuse me," I interrupt Paige. "I need to steal her away for a few minutes." I'm already pulling her away, and Paige doesn't stop me. She smiles knowingly before turning to her husband.

I don't look back as I pull Laney out of the full banquet hall that's been set up. I'm not entirely familiar with this place, so I take a couple of wrong turns before finding a semi-secluded area for us to talk.

I pull her in front of me and wrap one arm around her lower back and use the other to brush a stray hair off her face. I can't seem to stop touching her tonight—she feels too good in my arms to even attempt to stop. "What's going on in that gorgeous head of yours?"

Her eyes get sad before she blinks the look away and shakes her head, pasting on that fake smile I'm starting to hate. "Nothing. Just tired. It's been a big day."

"You've always been a shit liar, Laney. I don't know why you think you could possibly get away with it now."

She won't meet my eyes. "Doesn't it bother you, lying to them?" Her voice is quiet, less confident than it normally is.

"I'm not lying," I say, my voice soft, but not timid like hers.

She pushes out of my arms and glares at me. "Stop, Dom. No one is here but me. You don't have to lay it on so thick."

She really thinks I'm still pretending. Did that kiss not fuck her up the way it's fucked me up? Every look, every touch, the kiss earlier. None of that was fake for me.

But she thinks it was.

Fuck. I need to get us on the same page here. I open my mouth to speak, only for a voice to carry into our little hideout and a bunch of press to round the corner.

Shit.

They break out into smiles and rush forward. "Dom! Great game tonight, man."

"How're you feeling about next season?"

"How long have you and Alayna been seeing each other? Do you attribute your success tonight to her?"

"How does she feel about your scandal with Jen Summers?"

The questions rush at us, each of the reporters talking over each other. I need to get us out of here.

I hold up my hands, putting on my most affable smile. "Hey, hey, hey. Guys, come on. I already answered a bunch of your questions earlier. If it's not about the game, I've got nothing to say. My relationship is private."

"Ah, come on, man. Give us something!" one of the guys in the back says.

I open my mouth to double down on my initial response when I see Shawna behind the crowd. She glances at Alayna and then gives me a very pointed look. After a moment of us just staring at each other, she rolls her eyes and looks at the crowd of reporters to make sure no one is looking at her and then makes a kissy face before pointedly looking back at Alayna.

I swallow thickly. I know what she wants me to do. I just don't know how Laney will take it if I kiss her for the cameras right now. She already thinks I've been faking it when I haven't.

Maybe if I make the kiss different from our other kisses, she'll realize what's real and what's not.

I turn to Laney and gently cup her cheek with one of my hands. Then I bend down and brush my lips against hers, softly, tenderly. I can't quite keep all my burgeoning feelings for her back, but I still manage not to deepen the kiss like I want to. The clicking of cameras echoes around us, but I ignore it all to focus on her. When I pull away, her deep cerulean blues pull me in, wishing I could tell her what I was feeling.

But the look in her eyes stops me. There's a hint of sadness, but what's most prominent is resignation.

And it hits me like I've just been tackled by a 300-pound linebacker. My words will never be enough. I've told her she mattered for years and then took her for granted. I knew this, but somehow looking into her eyes drives it home.

No, this time my actions have to do all the work for me, and it's clear to me I've got a long way to go before she'll realize the truth.

When I look back at the reporters, determination sizzling in my veins, they all seem pleased, but none more than Shawna who's got a bright smile on her face and gives me a quick thumbs-up before she swoops around and tells the reporters they need to return to the press room.

"We should get back to the party," Laney says, her voice quiet but determined. She wants to keep me in the friend box because she doesn't think I love her the way she confessed to loving me.

But she's wrong.

And I'm going to prove it to her.

TWENTY-ONE

Alayna

Our fourth official "date" starts off as a surprise. Despite my wishes, Dom refuses to tell me what we're doing. I'm even more suspicious when he opens the back door of a black SUV and I see a driver. I shoot him a look and he just smiles at me.

"Get in, Sunshine."

I arch a brow at the nickname he rarely uses, but I know his determined look well so I do as I'm told. The drive doesn't last long until we start to slow because of hordes of traffic and people.

"Oh shoot. I forgot tonight is the Wrecked by Reason concert."

"The one you tried to get tickets to but couldn't, right?" he asks, not looking at me, but focused on where we're going.

"Yeah," I mumble, still salty about it. I've been a fan of the lead singer, Sloane Halloway, for years, well before she started the band Wrecked by Reason. Her songs got me through so many rough days, and I definitely played "When Will You See" more than once thinking about Dom. It felt like she'd written it specifically for me—a girl in love with her best guy friend and wishing he'd see what was always right in front of him.

I'm frugal with my money, but I would've splurged to see WbR if only the tickets hadn't sold out. And the resale tickets were astronomical—higher than could even be considered a splurge. They gave Taylor Swift a run for her money.

The driver stops, I assume to let people pass by because there are crowds everywhere I look, but then Dom undoes his seatbelt and opens his door.

"Good thing you're friends with a guy who's got connections."

He holds his hand out to me, and I stare at him wide-eyed and jaw on the ground. "No fucking way."

His smile brightens. "Yes fucking way. Now get your sexy ass out of the car so we can go see this thing."

I squeal and launch myself out of the car and into his waiting arms. He spins me around in a circle, laughing with me, and then sets me on my feet. I bounce on my toes and, without thinking, grab his face in my hands and plant a kiss on his lips.

His hands instantly tighten around me and he pulls me flush against him as he deepens the kiss. A groan escapes his throat, pulling me back to my senses as I break our kiss. My cheeks are hot, and I know they're likely bright pink. I can feel them get hotter when I see an expression on Dom's face he's never given me before. His eyes are filled with such a fierce hunger, it makes me breathless.

"Thank you," I whisper so quietly I'm not sure he hears me, especially when he just keeps staring at me like he wants to devour me. God, he's so much better at pretending than I am.

"Should we go in?" I ask a little louder, hoping he'll lose that expression on his face because it's messing with my head, and God knows my head's enough of a mess already.

"Sure," he finally responds, his voice deep and gruff.

He grabs my hand and leads me forward. Once inside, we make our way to a VIP section.

Throughout the concert, Dom is attentive and joins in on some of the songs with me. When Sloane sings "When Will You See" in homage to her early days, tears form in my eyes as I belt out the words. It's only as the song is wrapping up that I finally glance over at Dom, and all the air in my lungs evaporates at the longing in his eyes.

No, I must be reading him wrong.

Ripping my gaze away from his, I search for the only reason he'd look at me like that.

"What are you looking for?" he asks, leaning close to be heard over the shouts of fans.

I put my lips against his ear, hoping I won't be overheard and blow our cover. "The cameras."

He pulls back, a furrow on his brow, and then it morphs to something else, something sad but determined.

"As far as I'm aware, there aren't any. Not pointed at us anyway."

"Are you sure?"

"If there are, I didn't notice them."

Despite desperately wanting to be at this concert, I can't seem to look away from him as the next song starts.

"Dom..."

He leans down, his lips grazing my ear. "I'll sing it to you when you're finally mine," he says, mimicking the words in the song when her best friend finally sees her and declares his love for her.

My heart pinches, and I pull away from him, refusing to look at him. "That's not funny, Dom."

"I'm not laughing," he says, still standing painfully close to me, his nose nuzzling against the top of my head. I close my eyes as goose bumps break out across my arms and down my spine.

"Dom." It's a plea from the deepest parts of my heart. He can't do this to me, not now. Not like this.

He's just afraid of losing me. That's all this is. He might think he means it, but I know him—sometimes better than he knows himself—and I would never survive him making this real and then getting bored with me and wanting that party-boy-no-strings-attached lifestyle again.

He steps back and I open my eyes, laser focused on the action happening on stage. We don't speak for the remainder of the concert, but I can feel his large presence next to me the entire time, the tension growing with every second. By the time the show ends, my heart is racing and my nerves are lit up like it's the damn Fourth of July.

We walk quietly through the throngs of people and out into the cool Los Angeles night. The car we came in is parked out front, our driver waiting for us. He opens the door when we get closer, and Dom puts his hand on my back to usher me inside. His palm is scorching through the thin fabric of my shirt, and a hot pulse beats between my legs.

I need us to get back on solid ground. ASAP.

Two cold water bottles are waiting for us in the back seat, and I quickly pick mine up and down half of it.

"Thank you for tonight," I say into the deafening quiet of the car. I glance over to find Dom staring out the window, his reflection becoming clear as we pass under streetlights. There's a pensive look on his face, and that slight furrow to his brow that looks sexier on him than it's ever looked on anyone else. I start to question if he even heard me when he finally responds.

"You're welcome, but you don't have to thank me for doing something nice for you. It's the least of what you deserve." He turns his head, pinning me with his crystalline eyes. "You deserve to be spoiled every day, cherished every night, and loved every second in between."

I swallow thickly, afraid to speak and one hundred and fifty percent certain he can see my pulse hammering in my neck. I don't know how to respond. Honestly, all thoughts have been completely obliterated with that one sentence.

How the hell am I ever supposed to get over this man when he says things like that?

He rotates his body to face me as best he can with the seatbelt hindering him. "I have a lot to make up for, but you were unhappy with how things were. I heard you when you admitted your feelings, and you know I'm a guy who needs time to process big things like that. Just like I know you need time to adjust to change, especially when it's not a change you've planned for or fully believe is real." He leans closer, and I find myself leaning toward him. "But I can assure you, *this* is real."

He drops his gaze to my lips a split second before we both surge forward, our lips meeting in a hot kiss. His thick fingers slide into my hair, holding me tight to him as he plunders my mouth with salacious and toe-curling strokes.

I don't know if I believe him, but I know he's right about one thing.

This kiss is real—maybe the realest thing I've ever experienced. And it tempts me like nothing else could to throw caution to the wind.

TWENTY-TWO

Dominic

It took every ounce of self-restraint to drop Laney off at her place last night without following her inside and ravishing every inch of her.

It's been a long time since I've had sex—especially since Jen Summers's husband walked in on us before we actually did the deed—but even through my horny, lust-filled haze, I knew crossing that line right now when she's still set on pushing me away would be a bad idea.

She doesn't trust this—*me*—but she will. I'll prove to her I can be the man she's waited for.

I also know she needs some space. Laney thinks she knows me better than I know her, but she's wrong. I've made a study of her since that first group project in high school. I know when to back off so she doesn't double down with her stubbornness.

Which is why I'm heading to Ty's house today instead of going to her place like I really want to.

Ty answers the door with a smile on his face. He's the most affable guy I've ever met, and he totally fits the Canadian stereotype of a nice guy—something I'm sure his mom who still lives in Vancouver would be happy to hear. He can kick ass on the field and tackle hard, but then he'll get up and offer you a hand and a pat on the back with a sincere apology.

"Seems everyone had the same idea today," he says as he opens the door wider so I can step in.

"What do you mean?"

But before he answers, Romel walks from the kitchen to the living room with a beer in one hand and another that he passes to Gabe sitting on the couch.

I glance back at Ty, who just shrugs. We both head toward the living room, with Ty diverting to the kitchen to grab a beer for himself and a water for me, then we sit on the chairs across from the couch where Romel and Gabe sit.

"You guys wanna play a game?" Ty asks. "I've got Clue."

It's become a tradition for us in the offseason to have game night once a month, and somehow instead of playing something cool and sophisticated like poker, we ended up playing board games. Clue just so happens to be one of our favorites.

We move to the dining room table and get settled in our seats as Ty goes to his game closet—yes, he has an entire closet filled top to bottom with various board games.

"I'm surprised you're not with Kay today," I say to Romel, referencing his two-year-old daughter. Romel's wife, Sydney, died from cancer shortly after Kaylee was born. It fucked Romel up big-time, but we had his back and helped pull him through the worst of it. Now, he spends every spare second with that little girl; she's his whole world.

"She's spending time with Syd's mom today. A girls' day out, she called it." His voice doesn't catch like it used to when he says Syd's name. But it's also clear he's not fully on board with not spending time with his daughter when he's got the day off.

Ty comes back and sets the game on the table, grabs the remote for his stereo, and turns on Taylor Swift. We all smile, shaking our heads. We're secret Swifties, which isn't so much a secret since Laney knows and she spilled the beans to Danae.

Taylor Swift's latest hit plays softly on the radio in the background as Romel opens the box and shuffles the cards, randomly grabbing three before sliding them face down into the confidential envelope. Ty looks at his cards and then covers his clue sheet when he glances at Gabe, who's fighting back a smile as he tips his chin up, pretending to sneak a peek at Ty's sheet.

"No cheating! I know you peeked last time we played."

Gabe laughs. "No, I didn't. You're just pissed I figured out the clues before you did."

"Fuck off," he replies, but his usual grin fills his face.

"Where's Danae today?" I ask Gabe. Danae is the woman he hired to be his housekeeper after accidentally getting her fired from her waitressing job—even though he's one of the cleanest guys I've ever met. He fell hard for her, and they've been inseparable since they got together, but even more so after her stalker ex came after her not too long ago.

"She's hanging out with my sister," he says, taking a sip of his beer. "Where's Alayna?" he asks with an arch of his brow.

Fucker.

"Probably at home."

He chuckles from his chair next to me.

"What?" I ask.

Once he's finished marking off which cards he has on

his clue sheet, he looks up at me and says, "When are you gonna tell us what's going on for real with Alayna?"

I stiffen. "What do you mean?"

Gabe throws me a look. "Come on, dude. We know you better than anybody," he says, gesturing to the three guys around me. "And while we've all been betting on how long it would take you to see what was right in front of you the whole time—"

Ty cuts him off. "Hold up. You were completely unaware of anything remotely close going on with them until Romel and I pointed it out, and even then you didn't really believe it until even Danae saw it."

"Wait a second. You guys have been talking about my love life and my best friend?" I knew Ty had wondered based on our conversation when I had my revelation about my own feelings, but I didn't realize it was something they'd discussed together. They all kind of shrug in confirmation. "For how long?"

Gabe shakes his head as if he's shaking away my question. "It doesn't matter. The point is what's going on? Is this for real or what?"

I stare down at the cards in my hand and then put them face down on the table and rest my elbows on the edge. "You know my new PR rep?"

They all nod.

"Well, she wanted me to get into a fake relationship. I refused to do it unless it was with Laney."

Before I can even explain further, they all begin to get indignant.

"Are you fucking kidding me, Dom?" Ty asks, understandably outraged after the conversation we had before Laney and I started dating publicly.

"You really are an idiot," Romel says, shaking his head like he's never been more disappointed in me.

"Damn, man. Danae was really rooting for you two. Hell, so was I. I can't believe it's not real," Gabe says.

"Are you guys going to let me finish before you decide I'm a world-class idiot?" They gesture for me to carry on, so I do. "I said I would only do it with Laney, but before she even agreed, she confessed that she was in love with me. I don't know if she thought it would drive me away or what, but it had the opposite effect. It made me finally face my own feelings. I even talked to Ty about it."

Now Ty's in the hot seat. He shoots me a glare as both Gabe and Romel go off on how he could keep this from them. I swear, we're the fucking Golden Girls sometimes.

"Enough," I say, loud enough to be heard over their bitching and moaning. "I only talked to him about it first because he came over when I was feeling pretty low about the whole thing. I never planned to keep it a secret, but I've been focused on Laney. Once she agreed to this "fake" relationship, I knew I had limited time to prove to her that it could—and should—be real."

"So is it real now?" Romel asks.

I let out a heavy sigh. "It's real for me. Fuck, it's as real as it gets. She's the one. She's...fuck, I'm so gone for her it's not even funny. This is a total chick thing to say, but the first time we kissed, I knew I was done for."

"So what's the problem?" he asks, like he noticed that I emphasized it was real for me, but not for *us*.

"She doesn't believe my feelings are real. She thinks I'm doing this because I'm afraid of losing her, and she's partially right, but that's not the driving force behind my feelings. It's more like a result of them. *Because* I've finally realized I love her and don't want anyone else, I'm afraid to lose her."

Gabe frowns. "I think you need to go back to the beginning and give us all the details so we can help you figure this one out."

So I do. They listen intently, all of them on the edge of their seats, but serious expressions on their faces like they're taking it all in so they can give me the best advice.

On the field, I never doubt that these guys have my back, but sitting here in Ty's living room with them surrounding me, I know they'll have my back whether we're on the field or not. We're not brothers by blood, but by choice. And sometimes that's much stronger.

By the time I've finished, my heart is racing and my palms are a little sweaty. Romel, Gabe, and Ty all exchange glances, then Ty stands. "I'm going to order some pizza. I have a feeling we're going to be here for a while."

He moves to the kitchen, already pulling out his phone. Romel sits back, lifting his leg to rest his ankle on his knee as he stares at me, his eyes narrowed in thought. When Ty comes back in the room, Romel leans forward.

"Alright, here's what you're gonna do."

TWENTY-THREE

Alayna

There's a buzz in the air and it's not because everyone is on pins and needles about the results of the recent audit we had. Tessa walks into my office with a smirk on her face.

"You should hear everyone tittering away out there about the new celeb in our midst."

I drop my head to my hands. "Ugh, I didn't think about how this would affect me at the office."

"Relax. It'll blow over soon enough, but you had to know people would talk. It's the most exciting thing to happen to anyone in this company since ever." She drops into the chair on the other side of my desk. "How are things going with Dom?"

Before I can answer her there's a knock on my door and our boss, Stanley, peeks his head in. "Hey Alayna, you got a minute?"

"Sure thing, Stanley. What's up?"

He walks in, his smile growing into a Cheshire cat grin. "Well, I'm happy to report we passed the audit with flying colors, and it's all thanks to you. They were particularly impressed with our decision to pivot at the end of Q3 last year, which we wouldn't have done if you didn't suggest it based on the data you were seeing. So, I just wanted to thank you personally."

"Thanks, Stanley."

"We're lucky to have you, Alayna," he says before making his way back out the door.

Tessa and I look at each other, her eyes wide and her grin growing. "Did Stanley really come out of his office to *thank* you?"

I huff out a laugh. "He sure did."

Stanley is notorious for never leaving his office unless it's to play golf or time to go home—although there's a rumor that he sleeps on his couch more nights than not since his last divorce. He typically only talks to his assistant and his VPs. I'm surprised he didn't send his thank you through my direct supervisor, Clayton, which he's done before.

"We must have really rocked that audit."

"Well, that should lighten things around the office and maybe even take some of the excitement of your new celebrity status away."

There's another knock, and both Tessa and I look to the door at the same time.

"Or maybe not," Tessa murmurs as she stands and walks past Dom, throwing me a knowing smile once she passes him.

"Dom," I say, standing up and feeling suddenly unsure what to do with my hands, which is ridiculous because this is my domain. "What are you doing here?"

He holds up his hands and I now notice the large to-go coffee cup in one hand and the brown bag with something that smells heavenly in the other.

"I knew you were under a lot of stress because of that audit you guys had, and when you're stressed you tend to work through lunch and skip snacks, so I figured you'd be jonesing for a coffee and blueberry scone."

Blueberry scones are my favorite, and as I open my mouth to tell him that wasn't necessary, my stomach gives a loud grumble. Dom ducks his head, chuckling before peeking up at me, and the tender yet heated look he gives me sucks all the air from my lungs.

I'm thrust back to the concert two nights ago and more importantly the things he said to me before the scorching-hot kiss we shared in the SUV. My body heats at the memory of how his hands felt on my body as his lips claimed ownership of mine.

His smile slowly falls the longer we stare at each other, and I'm sure he can read every thought in my head—he's always been able to when he's paid enough attention.

"Thank you," I murmur. "That was thoughtful of you."

His smile is completely gone, replaced by a seriousness that I feel down to my toes. "It's literally the least I can do." He moves closer, not even having the decency to stay on the opposite side of my desk but coming to my side and closing the distance between us until there's only a foot of air between his body and mine. "I'm going to prove to you that I can be the man you need. That old version of Dom is gone and buried. This time, I'm sure of what I want, and I figure you deserve to know that what I want is you. Not just as my best friend—even though I want that too—but I want it all, Laney. And I don't want it with anyone else but you."

I swallow thickly, unsure what to do or say, but Dom takes care of that too. He sets the coffee and brown bag on my desk, then slides his fingers through my hair, cupping the back of my head, and gently, tenderly, brings my mouth to his in a kiss that has my knees turning to jelly. I grip his hips, close my eyes, and fall into the kiss.

I'm tired of fighting this, and I don't have the strength anymore to pretend this isn't everything I've ever wanted. Maybe it didn't start out that way, but I need to trust him.

He pulls back slowly, his blue stare fixated on my likely flushed face. He brushes his thumb along my cheek, then against my bottom lip, and that throbbing between my legs that only he brings out in me roars to life.

"Can I see you tonight?"

"Yes," I whisper.

One side of his lips tilts up in a lopsided grin that has my heart beating in double time. "Call me when you get off work and we can do something quiet tonight. Maybe pizza and a movie at my place?"

"Won't Shawna be upset that it's not visible for the press?"

"Tonight's not for Shawna. Tonight's for us."

Us.

He says it so definitively, and I fight against my own smile at how pleased I am that he doesn't want to go out and parade our relationship for the press.

It makes it more real, and for the first time since I agreed to our arrangement, I start to believe that maybe we could truly make this work.

My day gets even better when several hours later I get a call from Jared about my paintings that he's been displaying at his gallery.

"They sold out."

My jaw nearly hits my desk. "What?"

He laughs. "You heard me. I sold all five of them. Think you can paint some more? I had a few other interested buyers, including one who was curious if you do custom pieces."

I'm speechless. Literally speechless.

"Alayna, you still there? Or did I lose you?" There's humor in his voice, and I can practically visualize him smiling knowingly on the other side of the phone.

"I'm here. I-I can't believe it."

"Well, believe it. I told you that you were talented. Maybe now you'll believe me. Hey, I gotta go, I've got a customer, but let me know when you can get me some more paintings."

"Okay," I say and then he hangs up.

Holy shit. I lean back in my chair and let my smile break free. A hysterical laugh pops out of my mouth. He sold my paintings.

Maybe I'm good enough after all—in all areas of my life.

TWENTY-FOUR

Dominic

Tension builds between my shoulders as I grip my cock and tug it with firm strokes, my eyes closed and my lips parted as I imagine Laney's hand in place of my own.

Four weeks.

That's how long it's been since our first kiss. And even though it's like no time at all, it feels like a goddamn eternity to me. I've never wanted a woman this badly, and it's turned me into a fucking wreck. We've kissed since, short goodbye kisses and deep, passionate kisses that make me harder than steel.

But I've not let it go past that—despite the fact I'm going out of my goddamn mind with wanting her. Our situation is still fragile, and when I take that next step, kissing every inch of her delectable body, I don't want her to have a single doubt about the honesty of my feelings.

So instead of doing all the things I want to do with Laney, I masturbate—sometimes multiple times a day—to take the edge off. And tonight I suspect I'm going to have a harder time than usual since we're going to a charity gala with a few other players from my team and I already know Laney's going to look fuck hot.

I grip my hand tighter around my cock, and I can picture Laney here on her knees, begging me to give it to her, her luscious pink lips parted and eager. My stomach clenches as pressure builds at the base of my spine. I imagine her pink tongue darting across the head of my dick before she wraps those perfect lips around me and sucks, her cheeks hollowing. My orgasm rushes over me, and my whole body goes stiff on my bed as thick jets of cum land on my stomach.

I sag into the mattress, my body barely feeling sated at all. A glance at the clock shows I don't have much time to get ready, so I try to shake off the disappointment of an orgasm that left me wanting and get in the shower.

It doesn't take me long to clean up and get dressed, but by the time I'm done, the town car that I hired for the night is already here. The drive to Laney's place is about twenty minutes, and I use that time to text Trey to see if he's heard any rumblings about what the Wolves might be thinking in regard to possibly trading me.

I'm hoping they don't, but I'm preparing myself for the worst.

I glance up from my phone as the town car pulls up to Alayna's place, and my mouth goes dry. I can barely pull my gaze away from the sight before me as I open the door and slide out of the car, my jaw dropped and my eyes scanning from her blonde hair that's hanging in soft waves past her shoulders, down the elegant red dress that accentuates her curves in a way that has me wanting to get on my knees and worship her existence in my world, to the black stilettos that match her clutch.

"Well? Is this okay?" she asks.

I can't even believe she has to voice that question. I try to speak, but my throat is tight. I clear it and try again. "You're perfect," I say, my voice coming out husky and giving away the impact she has on me based on the blush that coats her cheeks at my words.

"Thank you," she says.

My feet move without my permission, my whole body on autopilot to get as close to her as I can. When I get within touching distance of her, I wrap one arm around her lower back, while the other hand slides over her jaw, my thumb rubbing across her bottom lip before I replace it with my lips.

I love kissing her.

Kissing was never that big of a deal to me, but kissing Laney is the best natural high in the world. Although, even better than kissing her is the way she sways against me, leaning her gorgeous body against mine. She lets out a soft little mewl that has my dick straining in my pants.

Fuck, it's going to be a long night, but it's worth it.

She's worth it.

The charity gala tonight was my idea because I was sick of Shawna's shallow date recommendations. She wanted us to attend some kind of charity, and I knew Gabe and Danae were going to this one that aims to raise awareness and support for survivors of domestic abuse, so it felt better to support something I know they're both big advocates of than something that was just meant to be a publicity stunt.

I don't want my life to be a publicity stunt. I want it to have meaning. Maybe tonight, some of the undeserved star power I've received since the Jen scandal can actually do some good and bring attention to an important cause.

Laney takes my hand as we exit the car, and we walk the short path to the entrance of the hotel where the event is taking place. Cameras flash and questions get thrown at us, but I ignore them all. It's easier to do now that I know this thing with Laney is real.

Gabe and Danae are waiting for us right outside the banquet hall. "Were the reporters your idea?" Gabe asks.

"They come with the territory these days. Shawna likes a report of where we'll be when we're going out, so she can let them know."

Gabe frowns. "I'm surprised this whole thing hasn't died down yet."

Now it's my turn to frown. "Yeah, well, it might've already if it weren't for Jen, continuing to drop hints that she's still upset about the whole thing."

Which is such a load of crap. She doesn't care; she just likes the attention. I heard she's getting a lot of offers for prime roles that any up-and-coming Hollywood actress would kill for. Instead of killing a person, she's just trying to kill my character with subtle and vague social media posts and comments to the press when she's out. She doesn't say my name explicitly—she doesn't have to because the press makes their own speculations.

"Sorry you both still have to deal with all the craziness. I don't know how you do it," Danae says, looking over at the wall of photographers and flashing lights.

"It's not great, but hopefully it's only temporary," Laney says, and my shoulders stiffen with doubt. Does she mean the press will be temporary because they'll find something else to salivate over or because our deal will run out?

Maybe I'm not feeling as confident in our new relationship as I thought I was.

"Well, should we go in?" Gabe asks as he gestures to the double doors that lead into the event. We all nod and Laney and I follow him and Danae.

We pass through the double doors into a large room decorated with purple sashes and round tables covered with cream linens and purple table decorations. There's a silent auction set up in one-half of the room and a singer performing on a stage at the front of the room while people mingle or sit at tables. We make our way to a table and take our seats.

Danae and Laney start chatting and I overhear her telling Laney about a fundraiser that Will and Gina are doing for a local no-kill animal shelter where Will got his dog, Rex. Laney's always been a softy when it comes to dogs, so I start figuring out if we have any plans next weekend, so I can plan for us to go and support the shelter.

Dinner is served shortly after we're seated, and as the five-course menu comes to an end, several speakers start to get up and talk. Their stories are heartbreaking and infuriating. More than once Gabe and I exchange a look, both of us clearly thinking the same thing—that abusers deserve the worst form of karma possible. More than once I catch Danae wiping her eyes and Gabe pull her close against him. I know he found this charity because he wanted to support others who experienced the same terror Danae did. Both of them have a lot to work through over that trauma, but I have no doubt they'll get through it together.

After the third speaker, Laney grabs my curled fist. Her touch immediately soothes the grated nerves of hearing the hell these women—and surprisingly one man—went through.

"You're so tense, I'd think you were made of stone," she whispers against my ear. The heat of her body touching me has my shoulders falling and my body relaxing.

"I don't like hearing about these people suffering this way."

She cups my cheek, staring at me with so much love in her eyes, there's only one thing I can do in this moment. I lean forward and kiss her. Our lips brush with a tenderness I've only experienced with her, and it's something I'm quickly growing addicted to.

When she pulls away, her ocean-blue eyes shine with sincerity. "You're a good man, Dominic Smith."

I want to believe her with everything in my soul, but I haven't been a good man this past year, and not even she can deny that.

"I want to be."

Her lips curl up in the slightest smile. "You *are*," she says again before her gaze turns more vulnerable. "I wouldn't love you so much if you weren't."

It's the first time she's said it since she first confessed her feelings to me.

I drop my forehead to hers, soaking in her warmth—my Sunshine. I almost say the words back. I can feel them on the tip of my tongue, but something holds me back. It's not that I don't feel them, but I'm still not sure she'd entirely believe me. When I say those three words to her, I don't want her to have a single doubt about me—or us.

"I promise to always do everything in my power to be worthy of your love," I say instead, hoping someday—very soon—I'll be able to confess that her feelings aren't one-sided.

That all my love has always been hers.

It's impossible to keep my hands off her throughout the

night, and by the time I drop her off at her apartment, I'm so hard I could cut glass.

Fuck, I want her.

Even if it's just a taste.

She looks at me from under her long lashes. "Do you want to come up?"

Hell yes!

Instead, I try to play it cool and tell the driver to hang out for a bit. He's being paid a hefty sum for the night, so I don't feel bad about leaving him down here while I go up to Laney's apartment for a bit.

When we get inside, she sets her purse down and takes her coat off, her movements a little stiff, like she's unsure what to do.

I've got some ideas.

Walking up behind her, I place my hands on the wall on either side of her and bend down to kiss her exposed neck. She tilts her head to the side on a soft sigh, giving me more access, and I trail kisses up and down until goose bumps spread across her creamy skin.

"You have no idea how fucking gorgeous you are, do you?"

She spins around, her eyes glazed with a lust that matches my own. "Tell me."

Instead, I show her. I've never been very good with words anyway. I take her hand in mine and pull her to her bedroom. Her gaze never leaves mine as I reach around behind her and slowly pull her zipper down to the base of her spine. I slide my pointer finger up her spine until I get to the base of her neck and then I take both hands and slowly move to pull her dress down over her shoulders.

But she stops me. "What are you doing?"

I lean forward, kissing her. "I want a taste."

She gasps, but she can't honestly be surprised, can she? The sexual tension between us has ramped up with every date, every touch, every kiss. If I don't taste her pussy soon, I might literally die.

That guarded expression comes across her face, and I know Laney well enough to see the insecurity behind her eyes. She's always been a little self-conscious about her body, even though I don't think she has any reason to be.

She's fucking perfect. Every beautiful inch of her.

But that's okay. I know how to get her out of her head. And honestly, it's probably for the best I don't get her naked tonight or I might cave and fuck her until neither of us can move.

Instead, I guide her to the edge of the bed where she sits and I drop to my knees.

Her hands instantly go to my shoulders. "What are you doing?"

I smile wide. "I'm eating dessert."

Then I lift up the skirt of her dress and dive between her parted thighs.

She sucks in a sharp breath, and I glance up to find surprise in those blue eyes I want to get lost in for the rest of my life.

I rub my nose along the crotch of her nude panties, inhaling her musky scent. I place a kiss there before reaching up and pulling her panties down. She watches me with bated breath as I pull them down her legs and then throw them behind me.

Not wanting to break eye contact, I push her dress up until it's bunched at her hips and then, watching her every reaction, I lean forward and lick up the seam of her sex to that swollen bud at the apex. A groan escapes as her flavor bursts on my tongue.

"So fucking perfect," I murmur before I dive in for another taste. I slide my tongue between her folds before circling her clit. Her fingers grip my head as her hips buck into my mouth and a moan breaks free from her.

Fuck, she's responsive.

It turns me on watching her get worked up, knowing I'm the one giving her all this pleasure. I slide one finger, then another into her wet heat, thrusting at a slow pace before slowly increasing the motion. All the while, my mouth stays suctioned to her clit which pulses against my tongue. She rises higher and higher until her legs clamp around my head, then she lets out a scream as her orgasm rips through her. Her pussy squeezes my fingers tight, and the sensation of her coming all over my face and fingers erases all control I had, and I come like a teenager in my pants.

She sags against the bed, her body limp and sated, her chest heaving. "Oh my God."

I kiss her thigh and then lean over her body and take her lips in a deep kiss that only skims the surface of the depth of my feelings for this woman.

"I'll call you tomorrow, okay?"

"Okay," she murmurs, her eyes twinkling and a soft smile on her face.

"Goodnight, Sunshine." I drop one more kiss to her lips because they're right there and I can't help myself, then I head to her guest bath to clean up the mess in my pants as best I can. Thankfully, my pants are dark and it's hard to notice the wet spot.

In the car on the way home, a rightness solidifies in my bones. I belong to her—now and always.

TWENTY-FIVE

Alayna

The dog fundraiser is set up at a local park near the no-kill shelter where I learned Will got his dog, Rex. We meet Will and Gina there right as the fundraiser is starting. This is a much more laid-back event than the gala we attended last weekend, with local food trucks parked on the street, a pet adoption fair going on, and a ton of little booths with miscellaneous activities. One has face painting, another is a dog groomer offering steep discounts to anyone who adopts a pet today. There's a band playing classic hits and little kids dancing around and blowing bubbles.

It's hard not to smile at all the happy faces—from both animals and people alike.

"Hey, let's check out that booth," Dom says, taking my hand and setting off a flurry of butterflies in my stomach. For the first time since we started this thing, the butterflies aren't because of his touch but because the booth he's pulling me toward just so happens to be Jared's.

After Danae told me about this event at the gala last weekend, I called Jared to see if he'd be willing to participate, even if he only used my paintings and donated all the proceeds. He was all for supporting the shelter because apparently all his animals have been rescues, and he likes finding new ways to give back to the community.

Which means the paintings that Dom is now perusing are mine, and he has no idea.

Or at least I didn't think he did until he turns to me with a glint in his eye that I know well.

"You've been keeping a secret from me."

My shoulders sag. "How did you know?"

He tilts his head and arches an eyebrow in that look that shouts *come on*. "No one knows you better than I do. I'd recognize your talent anywhere. I've stared at similar paintings in your apartment a million times. Hell, I've begged you to paint a ton for my house and even offered to pay for them."

"Yeah, but that felt weird because you're my friend. You have to be supportive."

His gaze grows fierce and he steps into my personal bubble until my head is tilted back to look up at him. "I'm not just your friend, Laney."

I can hardly breathe over the nerves that infiltrate my body. "What are you?" I whisper.

"I'm your man."

That doesn't clear things up enough for me. "What does that mean exactly?"

He grumbles, and my God, the way my lady bits tingle at that low, rough sound should be illegal. He slides his hand through my hair until his large, callused hand is gripping the back of my head and holding me close to him. "I'm your boyfriend, Laney. Only yours, for as long as you want me."

Then he dips his head to meet mine, and his next words

break through every last shred of defense I've held against him. "I'd like to be yours forever."

"I'd like that too," I confess because it's the truth. It's always been the truth. And I'm beginning to realize that I had no chance of successfully cutting him out of my life when our six months was up. It would've been like cutting out half of my soul.

He closes the small gap between us and kisses me fiercely, pouring all the emotions I've always wanted him to feel into our kiss.

A throat clears and we break apart, both turning to look at Jared who's got a huge grin on his face. "While I'm not a prude, this is a family event, so you two should probably tone it down." He can barely keep the laugh out of his voice.

Dom steps back slightly but wraps his arm around me, so we're still close. "How long have you been selling your work?" he asks me.

"Not long. It's kind of a complex turn of events. I went out to eat by myself when we weren't talking and met a waitress who chatted me up, and she's the one that said I absolutely had to meet her uncle who runs an art gallery." I point at Jared, so it's clear to Dom that Jared is said uncle.

"I met with him and he loved my stuff, so now here we are. This is the second batch I've painted for him."

"You sold out already?"

My cheeks grow pink but there's a flutter of pride in my heart. "Yeah. Can you believe it? Some random strangers actually bought something I painted."

His gaze gets soft as his thumb rubs circles where it rests on my hip. "I can absolutely believe it. I always said you were talented. So does this mean you're done in corporate America?"

"Nope. In fact, I just got a huge bonus for my role in our recent audit."

Dom's smile grows even wider, and the pride glowing in his gaze makes me feel like a million dollars. "Damn, Sunshine, just knocking it out of the park in all areas of your life, aren't you?"

This time it's my smile that grows wider. "I guess you're right."

He is. For the first time in a long time, I'm not just going through the motions. I'm trying new things. I'm kissing the man I've been in love with for years.

I'm thriving at life, instead of just showing up for the day-to-day that I got used to.

And it feels really fucking good.

I should've known something would come and knock the wind from my sails because nothing this good lasts forever.

The panel next to my door buzzes, and I glance down at my phone to check the time, but it's too early to be Dom. He should be here soon, but not this soon.

I walk to the intercom attached to the buzzer and speak into it.

"Yeah?"

"Hey, sweetie. It's Mom."

I drop my head to the wall and close my eyes. It's never a good thing when my mom shows up unannounced. I thought I'd left all her endless drama behind when I left Idaho, but Mom's always been the clingy type—to men, to money, to me. If she loses one, she clings even harder to the others. If she's here in LA, that can only mean she needs money, or her latest boyfriend dumped her.

Knowing my luck, it'll be both and she's here to beg me for a place to stay.

The last thing I need or want right now is my mom hanging around. I don't need her planting her poison in my head and messing with the fragile happiness I've found. But she's my mom.

Without saying a word, I buzz her in, already regretting it.

I wait for the knock on the door and then open it for her. She breezes in wearing a skin-tight black dress, looking like she's Audrey Hepburn in *Breakfast at Tiffany's*. She lets out a heavy sigh as she looks around my apartment. I'm sure it's much more colorful than she'd prefer, but growing up around neutrals became the bane of my existence.

Some days I really miss the mother I had when my dad was alive—the one that was softer and more down-to-earth. There was a realness to her that's been missing since that sheriff's deputy showed up at our front door, his hat in hand and an apology written all over his face. Sometimes it feels like both of my parents died that day. The woman who rose from the ashes of my father's death was not a woman I recognized. She was cold, needy, fake. She latched on to men who would provide for her everything she could ever want, except the one thing I knew she needed. The one thing we both needed.

Love.

But love is a real emotion I don't think she's felt since my dad died.

"Sweetie, you could do so much better than this small little place." She tsks.

My apartment is considered large—certainly larger than

one person really needs—by LA standards. It's expensive enough that she should be thrilled her daughter can afford such luxury on her salary.

"So what brings you to LA?"

She spins around, a smile blooming on her face, except only her mouth moves—thanks to Botox most likely. "You, of course! Well, I needed a little work done, and the best doctor is down here, so I thought, two birds one stone, you know." She flicks her hand dismissively.

It shouldn't hurt that she isn't really here to see me—it's exhausting being around her for any length of time—but the little girl that lives inside every woman aches with longing for a mother who would come to visit her daughter first, instead of being here for unnecessary surgery.

She looks me up and down, her look turning calculated. "You're dressed up. Perfect. You can take me out to dinner. I have some very exciting news to share with you." She leans closer, dropping her voice like she's spilling a secret she doesn't want overheard despite the fact no one else is here. "I met an amazing man, and he's here in LA!"

She *always* meets an amazing man—amazing until he drops her like a hot potato. And if he's in LA, does that mean she's not just here for a visit, but lives here now?

I rub a finger along my temple. "I thought you were still with Patrick."

She spins away, moving farther into my living room. "Oh honey, no. I could've sworn I told you ages ago. He was too old for me anyway. I need a more virile man, if you know what I mean." She spins around and winks at me before focusing back on the pictures on my wall, while I fight against the urge to vomit.

The last thing I want to think about is my mom's sex life.

Gross.

"I saw some tabloids recently...quite a juicy story in fact...about you and Dom." She glances at me and studies my expression before bursting into laughter while I remain frozen. "Oh my gosh. You didn't. Sweet girl, that is not a man who will be faithful. Trust me, honey. I should know. I've had my fair share of athletes. They're hot in the sack, but they can't be faithful to save their lives. It's not really their fault. All that testosterone and the attention they get in every city. Who could say no to women throwing themselves all over them?" Her gaze scans me from head to toe, and by the twist of her lips, she finds me lacking.

My stomach knots.

"Sweetie, you know I love you, but a man won't be faithful to you if you don't cut back on the carbs or hit a gym. If Brad Pitt could cheat on a woman as beautiful as Jennifer Aniston then none of us are safe, but especially not someone so...*curvy*. I could recommend my plastic surgeon for some lipo, but I really think you're reaching out of your league with Dom."

She walks toward me, graceful as a movie star walking the red carpet, and puts her palm on my cheek in a tender gesture that's so at odds with the vicious words that just left her mouth. Can she see the gaping wound from the metaphorical knife she shoved through my heart? As if I needed her to add doubts to what's going on with Dom and me when I was finally starting to feel like I was on solid ground with him.

"You know I'm only this honest because I love you and don't want to see you heartbroken, right?"

I swallow all the emotions bubbling up. "I know, Mom."

There's a knock on my door, and despite worrying about

who got into my building without being buzzed up, I'm grateful for the interruption.

When I open the door, Dom stands there in a pair of dark slacks and a white button-down with the sleeves rolled up to his elbows. A bouquet of red roses is held in his hands, and his face lights up when he sees me, the way it always does, except now I notice there's an added heat to his eyes when he looks at me.

He scans me from head to toe like my mom just did, but I already know based on how his expression morphs to blatant hunger that he doesn't find me lacking at all.

Not yet, at least.

I know I shouldn't listen to my mother's callous words. *I know.* But knowing and doing are two different things, and when the person who tells you something so awful is also the same person who's supposed to love you unconditionally, you question this kind of look from someone who doesn't have to love you at all.

Dom must notice something in my eyes—an emotion only he'd pick up on after years of knowing all my tells— because he starts to frown before his gaze shoots to movement behind me. I watch his whole face shutter when he sees my mom before he glances back at me.

"Mrs...Sorry, I don't know what you're going by anymore."

"Oh please, Dom, I told you ages ago to call me Cynthie. Hell, a man as handsome as you, I'd let you call me Cyn," she says seductively like her name could have two meanings.

I'd roll my eyes, but nothing surprises me about this woman anymore. Certainly not her blatant perusal of the man she just told me I wasn't good enough for because I'd never be able to keep his interest.

"Sorry, Mom, but I can't hang out with you tonight. Dom and I have plans."

She pouts, but like everything else about her, it's fake. "Oh, but honey, I'm only in town tonight. I leave tomorrow."

"You flew to LA for one day?" Dom asks.

She laughs that gratingly fake laugh. "Oh, you're too funny, Dominic. No, no. I got here about two weeks ago, but I spent that first week with Frederic, my new man, and then the second week recovering from a procedure. Got a little nip/tuck. You know how it is."

"'Fraid I don't." He steps closer to me, his body heat warming me where her words had left me cold.

Her smile wilts slightly before she forces it to be even brighter and refocuses on me. "Well, anyway. Frederic is flying us out to the Maldives for at least a week, maybe longer. I'll try to reach out when we're back in town. Alright, sweetie?"

So she really does live in LA now, at least until things with *Frederic* die down. Then again, maybe it's a permanent move since she's probably gone through all the available bachelors in Idaho. "Sure thing, Mom."

She sweeps out of my apartment as quickly as she arrived, and it amazes me that she can eviscerate me in such a short amount of time.

TWENTY-SIX

Dominic

I've always hated Laney's mom, but I hate her even more for that hollow look she's left on Laney's otherwise gorgeous face.

What a bitch.

I'd chase after her and give her a piece of my mind, but Cynthie thrives on the drama and attention. The best way to punish her is to pretend she doesn't exist.

So I do just that and place a warm hand on Alayna's back, rubbing a gentle circle until her stiff body relaxes and she leans against me. But that only lasts for a second before she stiffens again and moves swiftly away from me.

"Everything okay?" I ask softly, knowing it's not but hoping she won't shut me out. I know her mom always fucks with her head, but she doesn't usually pull away from me when that happens. Instead, I'm typically the one she runs to.

She clears her throat, but doesn't look at me. "Yeah, it's fine. Let me just grab my coat and we can go."

She's lying, but I'll let her. For now.

She's quiet for the entire drive to the restaurant where

we're meeting several of our friends. I assume she'll put on her game face when we get there; she hates for anyone to know she's ever negatively affected by things.

But her smile is brittle and her eyes are distant when we greet our friends. Jack Fuller, our star quarterback, is here with his pregnant wife, Paige. Will Edmonson, one of our wide receivers, stands next to his fiancée, Gina, a protective arm around her waist. They're planning a big wedding later this summer. Matt Fischer, a tight end, is chatting up Luke Carter, one of our fullbacks, while their fiancées, Nikki Denton and Emma Delaney, stand nearby laughing about something. Nikki's hand rests protectively over her small baby bump, and Matt has his arm wrapped around her back. Right next to them is the rest of the Fierce Four, Gabe with Danae, Tyler, and Romel.

We all order appetizers and beverages—most of us noticeably avoiding alcohol. Everyone seems in good spirits, but the longer the night goes on, the more tense I become. I'm about to lean over and ask Laney to step outside with me so we can talk about whatever happened with her mom when Luke stands up and taps his glass, getting everyone's attention from the various side conversations happening.

He's got a shit-eating grin on his face as he glances down at Emma who's mirroring his smile before he turns back to us. "Emma and I have an announcement. We eloped in Hawaii!"

Emma holds up her left hand, and it's only now I notice the thin wedding band that's joined her engagement ring.

The table breaks out in chaos. Shouts of congratulations and laughter abound. In the midst of all the excitement, I glance over at Laney and notice the vibrant smile that's taken over her face. I suck in a sharp breath as I stare at her in awe. She's always been beautiful, but right now, she's goddamn stunning. She leans forward, reaching out to hold Emma's outstretched hand and gushes over her. The excitement is only slightly tempered when the waiter delivers our appetizers and takes our meal orders.

When Matt starts hassling Luke about not being invited to the wedding, Luke speaks loudly enough to be heard over everyone else. "Well, we thought of that actually. We're holding a reception in two weeks and would love for you all to be there. I know it's kind of short notice—"

"We'll be there," several people say over him, Laney and me included.

We both glance at each other, smiling, but that smile slowly drops from her face as her eyes become more worried and distant. My gut clenches.

I wish she'd tell me what her mom said to her. I know it couldn't have been good, and I can't help thinking it had to do with me. The last thing I need is her mom planting doubts in her head.

I've done that enough myself, and I thought we were finally moving past that.

Emma gives everyone the details, and Laney pulls out her phone to add it to her calendar.

Our food arrives and I quickly separate the mushrooms out of my meal, putting each individual one I find on a small side plate. I hate mushrooms, but I like the flavor they add to the sauce on this dish, and instead of asking for them to be removed, I always save them for Laney because she loves mushrooms. I pick up the plate and pass it to her at the same time that she hands me a similar plate with the tomatoes from her salad—something she hates that I love.

"Thanks," I say.

"Uh-huh," she murmurs, licking a bit of dressing off her thumb and ensnaring my gaze. Her pink lips are tantalizing, but nowhere near as provocative as the way her tongue slides out to lick the rest off. She's completely unaware of how sexy she is and it's a goddamn shame.

Once again, I'm angry at myself for all the time I've wasted. All the time I could've spent worshipping her, building her up, telling her every day how beautiful, smart, and incredible she is. She's right that I've been a lousy friend, but by not noticing her for what she's truly always been, I'm a lousy man.

She's everything, but more importantly, she's *my* everything.

Swallowing thickly, I tear my gaze away from her lips. When I look up, Emma's staring at me with a smile on her face and her eyes bright with happiness.

"So when are you two getting married?"

Laney freezes next to me, her gaze shooting up from her plate to me and then Emma. "What?" she chokes out.

"Well, it took you two long enough to get together. And you know each other better than anyone else. When it's right, it's right," she says, that dreamy look taking over as she glances at Luke next to her. He smiles back, his gaze just as dreamy, and squeezes her hand on the table.

"We're taking it slow," Laney blurts. "Sometimes, it doesn't work out going from friends to lovers, ya know?"

Emma frowns and glances at me, but all I can do is stare at Laney, my chest feeling tight and my stomach swirling with unease.

What the hell? We're back to this again?

Fucking Cynthie. This is her doing, I know it. Laney had let her guard down and she said something shitty that now has her back to playing like a scared rabbit. But no more. I'm not letting her sabotage what we have, and certainly not because of whatever stupid lies her mom planted in her head.

I bide my time until everyone is distracted chatting and then I lean over and whisper into Laney's ear. "Meet me in the hall in two minutes."

Then I get up from the table and march to the hallway. I lean against the wall, waiting, and I swear those two minutes take a goddamn eternity. Then she rounds the corner, and like my nickname for her implies, it's like the sun breaking through my gloomy mood.

I'll never forgive myself for taking so long to notice her.

She reaches me, and I pull her into the closest single occupant bathroom. There are two, so I don't feel so bad stealing one.

"Dom, what the hell are you doing?"

"What are *you* doing?"

She frowns. "What do you mean?"

"You're putting up your walls again, Laney, and I thought we were done with that shit. Why would you tell Emma that we might not make it?"

Her eyes flash with indignation and she puts her hands on her hips, her stubborn streak shining through. "Because it's true. Just because we were friends before we got together doesn't mean it's a guarantee that this relationship will work."

"Have I given you any reason since we got together to doubt me?"

She crosses her arms over her chest and can barely look at me. "No."

Thank God. Because if I did, I'd beat myself up over it. "So, what's this about? And don't lie to me because I suspect I already know."

She nibbles her bottom lip, and when she looks up at

me, her eyes shine with the hint of tears and way more vulnerability than I expected her to give me right off the bat. "What if you get bored with me, or I'm not enough for—"

"I'm gonna stop you right there because whatever bullshit is about to come out of your mouth is just that." I step closer, holding her face with my hands and making sure she doesn't look away from me. "Laney, *I'm* the one who isn't good enough. Who will never be good enough. You are perfect for me and everything I wanted before I let that shit with my dad poison my ideas about love and relationships." Her eyes flare a little and I know what she needs, what I hope she's finally ready to hear, because the words have been clawing and scratching to get out for days—weeks even.

"I love you, Laney."

Her lips part, but no sound comes out. One single tear escapes her eyes as she stares at me wordlessly.

"I'm in love with you. Please believe me because it's the truest thing I've ever said, and I don't—"

She cuts me off with her lips surging against mine and her arms wrapping around my neck.

When we pull apart after several minutes, I drop my forehead to hers. "I'm sorry. I didn't mean to confess that in a bathroom. I'd planned something more romantic."

She huffs out a laugh. "This was perfect."

We sit there, soaking in the comfort we can only offer each other.

"I love you too, Dom."

Her words wash over me, and I know we're back on solid ground.

TWENTY-SEVEN

Alayna

I complete the finishing touches on my latest painting, feeling lighter than I have in days. Dom's been doing every-thing in his power to erase the words my mom planted in my head—words I told him about eventually.

He's been pretty convincing. Whenever I have any doubts, he kisses me and tells me he loves me. Sometimes, he's even listed different things he loves about me. When he's not here to reassure me, I've found solace in painting and getting out my complicated emotions on canvas.

It's been a relief to find that making money off my art hasn't taken the joy out of it for me. I still paint for me, but now I'm not so afraid of sharing it with others.

I stand from my stool and step away from my easel in my guest room/office and cross the hall to my bedroom. My long satin gown hangs on my closet door. Satin isn't always smart when you're as tall and curvy as me because it doesn't hide a damn thing, but thank God for the invention of Spanx which will make sure everything looks smooth. The goldenrod-yellow color reminds me of the yellow dress Kate

Hudson wore in *How to Lose a Guy in 10 Days*, and is one of the main reasons I bought it. I've always wanted to make a man's jaw—specifically Dom's—drop the way she stunned Matthew McConaughey. I can already imagine the way his eyes will heat with desire when he sees me.

I check the time on my phone and rush to the bathroom since I'm already running behind. Dom will be here in a little less than two hours to pick me up for Luke and Emma's reception.

I can't believe they eloped.

I've never given much thought to my own wedding, but I think I'd be sad not having my friends there. There's a pinch in my chest knowing my dad won't be there to walk me down the aisle. Maybe that's the main reason I've never spent much time thinking about it.

I rush through my shower, shaving everything and exfoliating my skin until it's soft and pink. I do my hair and makeup and then finally pull on my Spanx, shimmying my wide hips into the restrictive material. I slip the dress on last, then stand in front of the mirror admiring how svelte my figure looks.

The doorbell rings and I take a deep inhale to calm the quick flurry of butterflies in my stomach before heading to the door. When I open it, I'm greeted by Dom's large, imposing frame in a pair of navy dress pants with a white dress shirt that's stretched taut over his bulky shoulders.

But it's his electric-blue eyes simmering with an undisguised heat that has my breath catching.

His gaze slides down my body like a lover's caress, leaving goose bumps in its wake before it slides back up and locks on my eyes. His reaction is everything I've always wished for, and yet somehow more perfect than anything I ever imagined.

He swallows thickly, his Adam's apple bobbing. "You look"—he shakes his head and then says, his voice ragged and deep—"gorgeous."

It's such a simple word, but it bolsters my confidence and makes me feel lighter.

"Right back at ya, Ace," I say, trying to lighten the heaviness that's building between us. Then I wince when I realize what I said. "I mean, handsome, not gorgeous. I mean guys can be gorg—"

His widening smile cuts me off, and I feel a blush stain my cheeks. Only Dom can make me feel both insanely confident and a stumbling fool.

"You ready to go?" he asks.

"Yep." I grab my clutch sitting on the small table I keep near my door and step out, locking the door behind me. When I spin around, he holds out his elbow, with a soft smile on his face that always makes the butterflies in my stomach flutter wildly.

I place my hand in the crook of his elbow and let him lead me down to his waiting SUV. I've touched Dom like this hundreds of times—hell, this is nothing compared to the way he's devoured my pussy several times over the past couple of weeks, never letting me return the favor—but there's a feeling in the air tonight that I've never experienced, and if I'm honest with myself, it both terrifies and thrills me.

We talk a little on our drive to the venue, but mostly sing to the songs on the radio and laugh at each other's bad singing voices. When we pull up to the valet stand, my smile is glued to my face and I'm drunk on happiness—the kind of happiness that only comes from spending time with the people, or person, who gets you the most.

The reception is already in full swing when we arrive.

We easily find most of the football team standing near the dance floor where Luke and Emma are completely lost to each other. The way he looks at her makes my heart swell in my chest. That's a true, devoted love if I ever saw it. When I look up at Dom, he's already staring down at me, his gaze saying the words he's said to me every day since the restaurant bathroom.

I can't believe he's really mine and that he loves me.

"Dom!" We both look over to see Ty standing near Gabe and Danae, waving us over.

"Where's Romel?" Dom asks when we get closer.

Ty points out to the dance floor, and my heart nearly melts into a puddle at the sight of Romel dancing with his toddler daughter in his arms. Her eyes are bright with such a youthful happiness, and for once, a smile lights Romel's face. It's a rare sight since his wife died.

We all stand and watch them for a minute before we engage in our own conversations—Danae and I chatting while the guys talk about football. You'd think in the offseason they'd take a break, but I learned quickly that these guys live and breathe the sport, even when they're not playing it.

Eventually, Gabe interrupts us to steal Danae for a dance, and I'm about to go grab something to eat when Dom holds his hand out to me.

"Dance with me?" There's a gentleness in his voice he doesn't use often, but always makes me soften toward him.

"I'd love to," I say, placing my hand in his. He wraps his warm hand around mine and pulls me out onto the dance floor at the same time the song changes to a slow ballad. The heat of his palm sears through my dress on my lower back as he places it there and pulls me tight against his body, and gives me that same hungry look he did when I first opened my door tonight. Instinctively, I wrap my arms around his neck, our bodies practically melded together now.

We sway to the slow, sultry beat of the song, my pulse quickening the longer we stare at each other. No one else exists, both of us lost to each other. His normally crystalline-blue eyes darken and smolder, making me feel like prey that's been caught by the big bad wolf. His head dips down slowly, as if he doesn't want to spook me, until he rests his forehead on mine.

"I want to kiss you so bad," he murmurs, his voice low enough I know no one else heard him.

"What's stopping you?"

"Because Sunshine, I won't be able to stop at a kiss. Feeling your sexy body pressed against mine is doing things to me."

"What kind of things?" Is that my voice, all breathy and hoarse?

"Naughty things. So naughty, there's no way you'd ever confuse us as 'just friends' afterward. You'd be mine, just like I'm yours."

Lust makes my mind hazy, but my mom's voice whispers in my head. Can I ever keep someone as magnetic as Dom? It threatens to break into this happy bubble, but then he nips at my earlobe, just enough for heat to slice through me like fire and pool in my now soaked panties.

"Get out of that pretty head of yours, Laney. I love you. Be here with me."

"I'm sorry. I don't mean to let my doubts show—"

"I don't want you to have doubts at all. I want you to trust me when I say that I've been blind and stupid for long enough. I'll never go back to that. And now that I'm seeing my whole future with perfect clarity, all I want to do is go forward."

"With me." It's not really a question. He's right; he's made it clear how he feels.

"Only you. It's always only ever been you, and it'll only ever *be* you."

"I believe you," I whisper, the words surprising me with how true they are. Dom's love shines brighter than my mom's vitriol.

He studies me for only a second longer before he slides his hand down my arm, clasps mine in his big hand, and then pulls me toward the exit. He passes our table and grabs my clutch and then keeps walking.

"Shouldn't we say goodbye?" I ask.

"No."

"Dom—"

"I'll text Luke later, but he'll understand." He glances back at me and gives me a look that dares me to question him. I know that look of determination on his face means he will not be swayed, so I keep my mouth shut and let him lead me to the car.

The drive back to my condo is heavy with the weight of our combined lust to the point where it's nearly suffocating. By the time he parks, my skin feels like it's sizzling from how desperately I want him. He takes my hand as he walks us to the elevator and then hits the number four. The doors close—more slowly than I've ever noticed before—and the second they touch, he spins me around and pins me to the wall. His lips devour mine, his hands moving into my hair, while I wrap one leg around his hip through the slit in my dress, our pelvises grinding deliciously against each other.

He rips his lips from mine and slides them down my jaw to my neck, kissing and sucking all the way. My panting breaths are the only sounds I can hear over my heart hammering in my ears. Then he sucks on my pulse point at the same time one of his hands glides down the side of my leg and slowly pulls my dress up enough to slip under it.

Ding!

Oh, fuck me. Couldn't the damn elevator go slower? I'm in the middle of the hottest moment of my damn life.

He groans but pulls away, straightening my dress quickly before the doors slide open. Without a word, he grabs my hand and hauls me out toward my door. Once we're in front of it, he pulls me tight against his body and drops his mouth to mine, his tongue seeking entrance.

"Can't get enough," he murmurs between mind-bending kisses.

"Don't stop," I say—okay, beg—my hands running up and down his chest, hating every thread of clothing covering what I know is an incredible body underneath.

"Open the door, or I'm going to fuck you right here," he warns.

Is it really a warning if your body reacts in such a visceral way that he clearly just unlocked a new kink for you? I didn't think I would be into public sex, but my body is on fire and the idea doesn't sound half bad.

"Sunshine," he growls, and I swear his voice incinerates my panties.

I spin around and fumble with my keys while he continues to pepper kisses on the back of my neck. Finally, I get the door unlocked and shove it open as I spin around and find his lips already moving toward mine. We stumble inside, our lips locked together, our hands roving over every inch of each other's body.

Then his hand is sliding under my dress again, moving up, up, up toward that place I'm so desperate for him, when suddenly, he stops and pulls his head back staring at me with his lips tilted up ever so slightly, but confusion in his gaze.

My eyes widen as I realize what's stopped his path to the glory land.

My motherfucking Spanx!

TWENTY-EIGHT

Dominic

What the hell is she wearing, and how do I get it off so I can taste her pussy like I've been dying to do since the moment she walked out in this sexy fucking dress?

Her gaze widens and her cheeks turn a dark pink with pure mortification. She covers her face with her hands.

"Ohmigod, ohmigod, ohmigod," she murmurs to herself, shaking her head. "Um, I need to go to the bathroom and then we can...um, continue."

I grab her arm, stopping her from pulling away from me. "Nah, no more hiding from me, Laney."

She's too focused on her embarrassment—although she has nothing to be embarrassed about; it could be a chastity belt and it wouldn't make me love her any less—to notice me pulling down the zipper of her dress.

With a small smile, I continue pulling down her zipper until her dress loosens and she pulls her hands from her face. There's a little shock, but mostly resignation as she lets her hands fall and the dress falls too, skimming down her perfect body and unveiling a tan undergarment that starts just underneath her bra and covers her body until halfway down her thighs.

She plants her hands on her hips. "They're Spanx, okay?"

I look at the garment again and then back to her beautiful deep-blue eyes. "And what's their purpose?"

"They hold everything in."

"What?"

She huffs—fuck, she's sexy when she's irritated with me —and starts pulling it off. She has to do a little shimmy when she gets to the top of her hips, which makes my dick harder than granite as I watch her lush, full tits jiggle. Then she pushes it off until it gets to her ankles and she steps out of it one foot at a time. When she stands tall again, she plants her hands back on her hips like she's expecting me to make some kind of comment, but my mouth goes dry as my gaze scans up her mostly naked body.

We've been friends for years, but I've never seen so much of her creamy skin before. Even when we'd go swimming, she'd wear one-piece suits. Although looking at her now, I have no fucking clue why. She's a goddamn goddess, her curves the perfect handful that make me eager to bury myself inside her and grip those full hips in my hands as I plunge deep.

"Dom?" It's the little note of insecurity that pulls my head out of the gutter to focus on her face. She's nibbling her lip, her eyes filled with worry, which I can't stand.

I step forward, wrapping my hands around her waist, and pull her tight against me as I kiss her, sweetly at first, then deeper, wanting to taste her and memorize the feel of her perfect body in my arms. She moans into my mouth, and I nearly blow my load right then.

I slide one hand up and unhook her bra, then pull back

enough to pull it down her arms and throw it to the side. As I stare at her, our gazes locked, our chests heaving from how badly we want each other, I slide my hands down her waist until I hit the edge of her underwear and slide them down her hips. I follow it down, getting on my knees, still staring up at her as her panties slip down to her ankles. I lift one foot delicately in my hand and then the other until I pick her underwear up and bring the delicate piece of lace up to my nose, inhaling deep and groaning in ecstasy.

I slip them into my pants pocket. "You're fucking perfect, Sunshine. You always have been, and I'm so fucking thankful I didn't miss this because *this*..." I drop my gaze to her perfectly trimmed pussy. "This is goddamn heaven."

Then I lean forward and swipe my tongue up her glistening slit. She chokes out a moan and grips my head tightly with her fingers.

"Oh God, Dom."

"Yeah," I growl. "Say my name while I taste this sweet pussy." I flick my tongue against her plump clit and suck hard, loving the feeling of her shuddering above me. Her legs quiver beside my head as I continue my ministrations until her whole body is shaking and she's crying out as she comes all over my face. Fuck, I love eating her pussy. I lick her clean, enjoying the small aftershocks that make her suck in a sharp breath, and then kiss my way back up her body, paying special attention to her stomach. I never want her to worry that she's not perfect in my eyes because she is. She's more than I ever imagined or knew I needed.

When I get to her lips, she claws at the buttons on my shirt. "You're wearing too many clothes."

"We can fix that."

I work on my pants while she continues undoing the

buttons on my shirt until I'm standing naked and hard in front of her. I grip my cock and pump it twice, aching for her more than I've ever ached for anyone.

It suddenly feels like everyone else was a complete waste of time when she was here all along. Not for the first time, I'm mad at myself for how blind I've been. How much I've hurt her over the past few years when she's had to see me with other women when I should've been with her the whole time.

I hate that it took me so long to catch up, but now that I know she's it for me, there will never be anyone else.

That, I can promise.

She moves forward, sliding her hand over mine where it's wrapped around my dick. I move my hands to her body, cupping a breast in one while the other wraps around her hip. My eyes close in bliss as I suck in a ragged breath while she grips my thick cock in her hand.

"Fuck," I growl.

"Time to return the favor," she says as she drops to her knees, but the second her pink tongue flicks out against the head of my cock, I know I can't let her do this. I pull her up into my arms and carry her down the hall to her room. She stares at me with an adorable furrow to her brow.

"Why wouldn't you let me suck you?"

I stop just inside her door. She's trying to look calm and unfazed, but I know her. I can see that insecurity slithering in her eyes.

I lean forward and kiss her lightly. "Because if you did, I would've come instantly. And the only place I plan to come tonight is inside you."

She swallows thickly, staring at me, but doesn't say anything else. I move into her room and place her gently down on the bed, then grab her leg and kiss every inch until

I get to her mound. Then I move to the other leg and do the same thing. She's squirming on the bed, her pussy glistening just for me by the time I kiss up her stomach, still avoiding the one spot she wants me most.

"Dom, please," she croaks out.

I sit up because I can't take much more either. Watching the effect I'm having on her is the most intense aphrodisiac.

I'm about to line myself up when I pause. I tip my head back and groan. "Fuck."

"What?" she asks, sitting up on her elbows.

"I don't have a condom."

"Oh, I do." She leans over and opens her nightstand, pulling out a condom that's definitely large enough for me. I clench my jaw, trying not to think about why she has magnums in her nightstand.

How many guys has she been fucking?

I thought she told me everything, but there's been no mention of any guys lately.

When I look back at her, she's fighting a smile.

"What?" I say...okay, maybe I snap it.

She arches a brow. "Jealous?"

My stomach tightens thinking about her with another man, and I realize with a sickening gut punch this is what she's felt every time I went off with another woman. If she only realized how unfulfilling they all were. She and I haven't even had sex yet, and it's already more satisfying than anything I shared with those women who meant nothing.

She sits up, putting her hands on my cheeks. "Tessa gave them to me...probably as a joke, or maybe she knew me better than I knew myself. I put them there when I got home."

I shake my head. "I have no right to be upset."

"But you are."

"Yes," I begrudgingly admit.

She smiles wider. "Does it make me a bad person that I'm glad I finally made you jealous?"

"Yes," I growl, but my own lips are tipping up. "Now I need to prove to you why no one else will ever satisfy you the way I will."

Her blue eyes darken. "By all means, give it your best shot."

I growl and then tackle her to the bed, her laughter lifting any heaviness from my unnecessary jealousy. "You think that's funny," I tease, which only causes her to laugh harder.

I tickle her sides before moving to that spot behind her knee I know is her most ticklish spot. She shrieks and twists beneath me in a lame attempt to escape, her laughter ringing in my ears as my own rumbles low.

Then she jerks her hips up and rubs deliciously against my rock-hard cock, and suddenly neither of us is laughing. We're breathing heavy, staring at each other with that heady weight pulsing between us that I've only ever felt with her.

"Dom," she whispers, but there's so much being said in that one word.

Don't stop.

Don't break my heart.

If only she understood that she's the one threatening to break mine every time she has a doubt about us. That she owns me—heart, body, and soul. But I know my words aren't enough, so I let my body do the talking.

I slide the condom on and then push slowly inside her tight heat, her body achingly perfect underneath me. Her eyelids grow heavy, and she moans as I push all the way inside her. Her nails claw at my back as I start thrusting in and out, fighting against how close she's already got me. I can't come after only a few thrusts. Not with her.

I need to make this so good, she'll never think of leaving me. We're meant for each other—we always have been.

"Laney," I say, my voice ragged, her name all but a prayer on my lips.

She surges forward at the same time that she grips the back of my head and pulls my mouth to hers. We kiss deep, our tongues gliding against each other as our bodies find their perfect rhythm, her pussy clutching my cock so tightly, it's almost too much.

I break our kiss. "Fuck, you feel so good."

I grip her ass and tilt her hips at the same time I adjust my angle. She sucks in a sharp breath before arching her back and tossing her head back.

"Oh God," she cries as her orgasm rips through her, squeezing my cock so hard, I have no choice but to follow her over the cliff.

My whole body shakes with my release, my arms threatening to give out, despite the hours I spend regularly in the gym. Fuck me, sex has never felt this way before.

After the last of my orgasm has wrecked through me, I push myself to the side and collapse next to Laney, careful not to crush her with my weight but not able to stop touching her either. She's quiet beside me, her chest heaving as she tries to catch her breath, her gaze locked on the ceiling.

I reach up and brush my thumb against the apple of her cheek before cupping her face and tilting it toward me. Her eyes are filled with emotions I can't quite name, and that scares me. I've always been able to read her moods, but I'm lost now.

"No regrets, Sunshine," I whisper.

She closes her eyes slowly and a tear slips out, sliding down beside her eye into her hairline. My heart stalls before restarting at a frantic pace. I lean over and kiss her lips softly, trying to convey all the love that's overwhelming me into that one soft kiss.

When she opens her eyes, the fear in her gaze slays me. "Please don't break my heart, Dom. I won't survive it."

I surge forward and kiss her harder. "I'm done hurting you. I'll show you, Laney. Just please don't give up on me."

She doesn't say anything, but she doesn't push me away, and for now that's enough.

TWENTY-NINE

Alayna

The bright light wakes me up first, then the heavy weight across my stomach jolts me awake further. My eyes snap open, and my heart races for a second as everything from last night comes roaring back. And that heavy weight across my stomach? It's Dom's arm, his head smooshed against the pillow. He holds me tight like he's afraid I'll escape while he's asleep. But this is my apartment. Where would I escape to?

I slide one hand into my hair and stare at my white ceiling. I can't believe we had sex. Finally. And not just any kind of sex—earth-shattering, toe-curling, mind-bending sex.

Holy fucking shit, it was incredible.

My cheeks flush as I recall every salacious detail from last night—the way Dom owned my body in a way I've never experienced before. There's a delicious ache in my muscles, but my mind won't stop spinning.

"I can practically hear your thoughts," Dom mumbles next to me, causing me to whip my head in his direction.

"What? How'd you even know I was awake? Your eyes are closed."

"Your whole body locked up. And I know you, know how you think, how you freak out. Stop it."

I open my mouth, but I have no good rebuttal. He's right; I was about to spiral into a freak-out and for no good reason. Things are good between us—more than good, they're perfect.

He opens his eyes, the crystalline blue piercing me. They soften slightly the longer he watches me.

Something about the quiet of the early morning and being snuggled in my bed makes me admit the truth to him. "I'm scared," I whisper.

His hand comes up to brush through my hair before resting on my neck, his thumb rubbing soothing circles on my jawline. "I know you are. So am I."

"What are you scared of?"

He leans closer and I shift so our foreheads can rest against each other. "I'm scared of losing you, Laney. Nothing means anything without you." He takes a deep breath. "I know you think this whole thing started because I was acting out of fear and that none of it was real, but you're only half right. The fear of losing you definitely forced me to confront what I've ignored for far too long, but I promise you, no matter how this started, it's been painfully real for me from the very beginning. I want you, not for a charade or for the press. I want you for *you* because I can't live without you, because you're my best friend, and the woman of my dreams who I was too afraid of losing to realize how perfect we could be together."

"This is real," I whisper, believing each word with my whole heart. Fear doesn't make them any less true.

He kisses me tenderly. "This is the realist thing I've ever experienced."

"Hello, earth to Alayna," Tessa says.

I sit up straight, not even realizing that I've been slouching, and my gaze snaps to hers. "What? Sorry, I zoned out. What did I miss?"

She smirks at me. "Did someone not get enough sleep last night?"

I don't miss the innuendo in her tone.

I drop my head into my hands and take a deep steadying breath before I look back up at her and word vomit. "I had sex with Dom last night."

She stares at me, her eyes wide. "Is that all? I mean, you guys have been together for a while, right? It's not like this is the first...oh my God, no way! That was your first time together?" I didn't think it possible but her eyes widen even more. "Holy shit!" She leans forward, her eyes sparking with a barely repressed eagerness. "How was it?"

I tilt my head and give her a look that she reads appropriately.

"Okay, okay, I get it. Not the thing to focus on. We can come back to that later. I guess the better question is why do you look like you're questioning your sanity?"

"He says it's real, and I believe him, but does that make me naive? I mean, Dom's been a player—and not just on the field—for years now. Is it really possible for a guy to flip the switch and suddenly be a loyal, dedicated, and perfect boyfriend?"

She leans back in the chair across from me, contemplating my question. "If it were anyone else I would say probably not likely and you're being played." I open my mouth to speak, but she holds up her pointer finger and arches a brow, halting the words before they get a chance to leave my mouth. "But this is Dom. Your best friend and the one guy who has always been there for you through thick and thin, even when he had his shithead moments. He was still there and had your back, so if he's gonna flip the switch, the only person I could see him flipping that switch for would be you. I also think you need to let go of the idea that he could be the 'perfect boyfriend.' No one is perfect, although *I* can be pretty damn close." She winks at me. "Dom is going to make mistakes and fumbles, just like you will. So he'll never be perfect, but he could be perfect for you. That said, you know him better than I do, so if you're having doubts, where do you think that's coming from?"

I run my fingers through my hair, digesting her words while trying to process my own conflicting thoughts. "Honestly, I don't even know. I was feeling fine this morning, but then out of nowhere I just got hit with the thought that maybe I'm stupid for trusting him—trusting this thing between us."

"This thing between you two was a long time coming. Everyone who's met you two could see it coming a mile away. So, what's really driving this?"

I don't have to think that hard about her question. "My mom said some shitty things when she came to visit."

"Your mom was in LA?" She raises her eyes to the ceiling before letting out a huff. "I should've known. You always get in a funk after she visits."

"She apparently lives here now."

Tessa's eyes go comically wide—again. "Nooo."

I nod and purse my lips. "I know."

"Ugh, that is the last thing you need. She will happily

sabotage your happiness. You need to talk to her, Alayna. You can't let her make you feel like this anymore, especially if it threatens your relationship with Dom. You two have come too far and you're too perfect for each other to let anyone get between you two."

I let out a heavy breath. God, I'm not looking forward to that conversation. "You're right. I know you're right, but talking to her is so hard. She twists everything so that she comes across as just being caring."

"I think that's a really polite way to say she's a manipulative bitch."

I bite back a laugh. "Something like that."

"Even if she doesn't listen to you, because we both know it's likely it'll go in one ear and out the other, I think you owe it to yourself—and to Dom—to talk to her. To get your feelings out there and lay down the law. If she can't support you and keep her shitty comments to herself, then she doesn't get access to your life at all."

"You mean cut her out for good?"

"I don't care if you share the same blood. Your family shouldn't treat you the way she does."

I glance out the window, processing and figuring out when I'd even do it. I'm not sure when she's supposed to get back from her trip, but I agree with Tessa. I've let this go on long enough, and I can't keep having her voice in my head threatening to poison my happiness with Dom.

"I'll call her tomorrow to find out when she gets back into town. Maybe take her out to dinner or something."

Tessa nods. "A public place is a good idea. But make sure it's one that will also give you some semblance of privacy from the press. You and Dom are still making headlines."

"That's a good point." Although thankfully, we're not

making nearly as many headlines as we were. Jen Summers has been quiet the past few weeks which means there hasn't been any drama to stir up.

Tessa looks down at her skirt before smirking up at me. "So about that bombshell you dropped... You're not gonna leave your girl hanging, are you?"

I let out a laugh. "Fine, yes, if you must know, the sex is off the fucking charts amazing."

"I knew it!"

I'm so thankful for Tessa's friendship. Everyone deserves a friend who's willing to tell you the hard truth that you need to hear, and then follow it up with something ridiculous like how great the sex is with your hot football boyfriend.

I wouldn't change a single thing about her.

THIRTY

Dominic

Every year, Laney and I take a trip together in the offseason, usually somewhere tropical. It started after I'd had a particularly rough season and she suggested we go somewhere sunny for a week and relax. Shortly after we got home, Laney was dealing with a shitty coworker, and I suggested we plan for another trip the following offseason so we could blow off some steam and she could get away from the bullshit. After that, it was just a foregone conclusion that at some point during the offseason we'd travel somewhere where we had zero responsibilities. We now plan our trips nearly a year in advance, and I'm still in awe that not only are we still going after she tried to end our friendship, but now we're going as a couple.

It's funny how quickly things can change.

When we arrive at the small villa I booked, Laney's jaw drops. "Dom, this is...wow."

I agree.

We've stayed in some pretty cool places over the years, but the view out of this one straight to the vast turquoise-blue ocean is absolutely stunning. I come up behind her and wrap my arms around her, holding her tight. Her body sags against me as the stress she's been carrying practically melts away. This trip couldn't have come at a better time. I know Laney's been struggling with all the press—she's not used to the spotlight like I am—and already I can tell she's more relaxed and content than she was when we were back in LA.

I drop a kiss to her shoulder and she shivers, which only encourages me to do it again, and then again on that spot where her neck and shoulder meet.

"Dom..." she trails off letting out a little moan as I suckle a spot behind her ear. "We should unpack," she says, her voice throaty and low.

Fuck, I love watching her get turned on. Kissing her wherever and however I want. Holding her against my hard body.

I love *her*. Plain and simple.

Spinning her around, I hold her tight, my arm wrapped around her waist while my other hand slides through her hair.

"I love you," I whisper against her lips before I kiss her. It starts soft, but as she melts into me, I can't hold back, and I release everything I'm feeling into our kiss.

Our lips fit like they were always meant to be together, our tongues sliding along the other in perfect sync. She slides one of her hands between us and rubs my hard shaft, eliciting a deep groan from me.

"Where's the bedroom in this place?" she murmurs against my lips.

"Fuck the bedroom. Let's get started breaking in every inch of this place, starting right here against the window where only the ocean can see the way I ravish you."

I kiss her hard again before stripping her out of her

sundress. Her fingers fumble with the button on my shorts, but she gets it undone quickly. I shuck them down, taking my briefs with them, and then grip my shirt at the back of my neck and pull it off.

She stares at me, her eyes dilated and that luscious bottom lip between her white teeth. "Why is it so hot when guys do that?"

"Do what?" I play innocent when I know exactly what she's talking about. If she thinks I haven't noticed the way that move always gets her eyes to roam all over my chest, then she's blind.

She shakes her head, a sexy little smile on her face, and then slides her short fingernails down my chest, through my six pack, along my happy trail until she grips my hard cock in her hand.

Tilting my head back, I let out another groan. "Fuck, Sunshine. I love how you touch me."

"How about how I lick you?" she asks.

By the time my head snaps forward to meet her eyes, she's already on her knees looking up at me like a little minx. Her pink tongue darts out across the head of my cock and then I'm completely lost to her as she worships me with her mouth. And worship is the only word that comes close because it feels like a fucking religious experience. Her perfect lips wrap around me, and she sucks before dropping down and taking more of me into her mouth until I hit the back of her throat.

Nope.

If she does that again, I'm going to come so fast it won't even be funny, and I plan to always make her come first.

Pulling her up off the floor, I kiss her deeply before spinning her around and planting her hands on the floor-to-ceiling window. I could lift her up and hold her against it as

I fuck her, but I know she'd be self-conscious about being too heavy and me dropping her. She'd get in her head and not enjoy the moment like I want her to, so I save that for another time when I have her too out of her mind to even think self-conscious thoughts.

And I can't deny the incredible view when she's in this position. Her ass is a goddamn work of art. I kiss down her spine, loving the small goose bumps that raise her flesh, and then I grab a condom from my shorts pocket off the floor and make quick work of sliding it on.

I fit my thick length at her soaking wet entrance and slide home. And home is exactly what it is—what *she* is.

My home. My heart. My everything.

"I'll never get enough of this," I growl as I pull out slowly and then thrust back in as deep as I can go. She lets out a cute little mewl, but it's not enough. I need her mindless with pleasure, and I know exactly what will get her there. Leaning forward, I continue to pump my cock into her while I wrap an arm around her waist and move my hand down to her clit. It only takes a few gentle but quick circles on her clit for her pussy to convulse and her to let out a deep moan as she comes. The pressure of her pussy gripping my cock pulls my own orgasm out of me, and I come hard, stilling inside her and shivering every couple of seconds as she experiences aftershocks that feel like heaven when I'm inside her.

"I love you too, Dom," she whispers, her head resting against the glass as she catches her breath.

She can't see my smile, but she can feel the kiss I drop to her shoulder.

A week in paradise with my woman can't get much better than this.

We're snuggled together on the couch, Laney between my legs, her head resting on my chest, my hand casually brushing through her thick blonde strands. She lets out a soft sigh.

"That feels so good," she murmurs. Her voice is sleepy and sated after the past three days of mostly sex. It's by far the best vacation we've ever taken together. I don't think I've ever seen her so relaxed and at peace.

It's made me rethink our plans for when we're back in LA in a few days. "I've been thinking—"

"Did it hurt?"

I smack her ass lightly and she giggles which brings a smile to my face. "No, smart-ass. Now, as I was saying. I'm thinking about talking to Shawna."

She twists, her belly now resting on the couch as she rests her hands beneath her chin and watches my face. "About what?"

"This plan to be out in the press. I think we need to let it drop. It was one thing when it was all supposed to be fake, but we're a real couple. We're going to be out and about on dates anyway. We don't need things staged anymore, and honestly, I'm sick of the whole dog and pony show."

"Are you sure?"

Her expression is unreadable, but I keep going. "Yeah. I have you. That's really the only thing that matters at the end of the day."

"But what about the Wolves? Wasn't this whole thing supposed to convince them that you're not a liability to their team?"

"Yeah, but if they can't see the changes I've made over the past couple of months, then I doubt another few months of a ton of press coverage will help things. Honestly, it might even make things worse."

"Do you think Shawna will really go for that? And what happens if Jen Summers decides to talk about it in the press again?"

"I'll keep Shawna on retainer, but I'd really like to be able to live my life and focus on what matters—you and football. In that order," I add with a kiss to her forehead.

She buries her face in my chest and mumbles something.

"What was that?" I ask with a grin.

She puts her chin back on her hands, her lips tilted up slightly but her eyes shining with a seriousness I haven't seen the entire time we've been on vacation.

"I can't believe we're really here—together."

I wrap my arms around her, holding her close. "Believe it because it's not changing. I'm not letting you go now. You're stuck with me for life."

Her smile grows, and I swear my heart skips a beat at how beautiful she is when she's glowing with happiness. "Happy to hear it."

THIRTY-ONE

Alayna

I upheld my promise to Tessa, but unfortunately, the conversation I needed to have with my mom was something that needed to be face-to-face. And she didn't get back from her extended vacation—although her entire life feels like an extended vacation—until a week after Dom and I got back from ours.

A sigh escapes as I think about the absolute bliss of that trip with him. It felt like the reset we both needed, and the calm that's been in our life since we got back and he talked to Shawna has made our relationship feel even stronger. It's also given me the strength to go through with this conversation.

I show up to the restaurant early so I can get my bearings before Mom shows up. I hear her before I see her, flirting with the male host who guides her to our table. He smiles at her in that placating way that tells me he probably gets hit on a lot, but my mom doesn't notice the undertones of his smile and keeps flirting.

I need to make sure he gets a tip for putting up with her.

"Oh sweetie, you are positively glowing! Have you gotten work done?"

Only my mother would assume I'm glowing because of plastic surgery. It's sad that she can't recognize I'm glowing because I'm happy and in love.

"I just got back from my trip with Dom. We were staying at a villa in Kauai."

"Oh, that's nice. But Hawaii has nothing on the Maldives where Frederic took me. Absolutely pristine beaches. And then because we were having such a great time, we extended the trip. It was pure heaven."

I don't miss how she took a dig at my own vacation to rave about hers. Why does it always have to be a competition? Why couldn't she appreciate that I had a good time on my trip with the man I've been in love with for years without diminishing it?

I adjust my cloth napkin on my lap. "Anyway, Mom, I'm glad you were able to meet up. I was hoping we could talk."

"About what, sweetie?"

Here it goes. I can do this. I can tell my mother everything that's been bothering me.

I open my mouth to speak, but she beats me to it with a frown at the table—the bread basket specifically. "You didn't have any of that while you were waiting for me, did you? Carbs will go straight to your hips, and you don't need bigger hips if you're set on keeping a guy like Dom."

"That." I shout—not on purpose, but because my thin patience has now evaporated. Mom's eyes widen. I lower my voice. "That, the nitpicking and underhanded comments about my weight or shape, that's what I wanted to talk about with you. It needs to stop."

She places a hand on her chest, looking absolutely

affronted. "Honey. I told you, I only tell you the truth because I love you."

My throat tightens and I hate—*hate*—the sting of tears in my eyes. "But that's not love, Mom. Love is making me feel like I'm enough, like I'm more than enough, like Dom would be insane to not appreciate me, not the other way around. Love is wanting your daughter's happiness, not planting doubts in her head that have no place being there."

I lose my battle with the tears, and several break free at once, sliding down my cheeks. I brush them away quickly. Mom stares at me, her expression blank and her eyes only slightly wider than normal. She glances down at her lap and then back up at me, a brow arched.

"I didn't realize that my brand of love wasn't good enough for you. You've never spoken to me this way before, and I can only think that Dominic has been planting these awful words into your head. I'm ashamed you would ever think I'm trying to diminish you. Honey, of course I want the best for you, which is why I share my opinion on matters of your life—to give you guidance."

The tears slowly dry up with each word out of her mouth. Each word delivered with poise and no emotion— like she's reciting the winning lottery numbers. I swallow thickly and stare at her, seeing her with a new perspective.

She's never going to change.

Which means asking her to isn't going to get either of us anywhere. For the first time in my life, I realize there really is no salvaging our relationship. I tried to stand up for myself, and she claims it's Dom planting thoughts in my head when it's *her* who's been planting poison for years.

"You understand, sweetie, don't you?" She says it like it's not really a question, but a foregone conclusion that she'll once again get her way.

"No, I don't."

She freezes, her glass of lemon water halfway to her mouth.

"I don't understand you at all," I continue. "And frankly, I don't think I want to. I can't keep doing this with you, Mom. I can't keep letting you poison my happiness. So, unfortunately, I'm going to have to ask you not to visit me anymore. I think it's best for both of us if we don't interact at all."

She sets her water glass down without taking a drink and throws her napkin on the table. "Well," she huffs. "I never thought I would be treated so poorly by my own daughter. And after everything I've done for you."

I feel guilty for all of two seconds before I realize this is another thing she does. She tries to guilt me for "what she's done for me" while completely ignoring all the really damaging ways that she's diminished me over the years. And those far outweigh the things she's "done" for me.

She stands up with a regal grace I've come to expect from her. "Goodbye, Alayna."

Then she walks out of the room, not looking back at me once.

I sag back in my chair, and the sudden sting in my nose is the first warning of the tears that pop up and streak down my face. I don't know what reaction I expected her to have, but putting the blame on me and then walking out without a backward glance wasn't it.

I'm thankful this table is tucked in the back and there are very few people at the restaurant. None of them have a decent view of me as I cry silently into my napkin, trying to pull myself together enough to leave.

When strong arms wrap around me, I pull the napkin

away and am greeted with the same blue eyes that have always comforted me.

"Dom?"

"Shh," he says, pulling me up into his arms before resettling us in my chair with me on his lap. He holds me close, letting me cry into his chest.

"What are you doing here?" I croak out.

He brushes a strand of hair off my face, his eyes holding infinite kindness and patience. "I knew today would be hard for you. I've been outside the whole time. When I saw your mom come out, but not you, I decided to come in and see what happened." He holds my face, brushing my tears away with his thumbs. "It kills me when you cry, Sunshine. What did she say?"

I shake my head because I'm not ready to break down the whole short but painful conversation. And like the amazing friend and boyfriend that he is, he doesn't pry. He just holds me and lets his strength seep into my body until all the cold I felt when my mom left is replaced by warmth and possibility.

This right here is love.

Whatever my mom thinks love is, she's missing out on the real thing.

/ THIRTY-TWO

Dominic

I've put this off long enough. Laney saw him calling me the other night—and me promptly ignoring said call—and told me I couldn't avoid it forever. She thinks I need to hear my dad out or else I might regret it when he's gone and I can't talk to him anymore. Her own conversation with her mom had her reeling for a few days, but then she admitted to me she was glad she did it because at least it gave her closure. She thinks I need the same thing with my dad. I don't know if she's right, but I'm sick of ignoring his calls, and I'd rather get this done and over with.

I pull up in my rented SUV outside his house. It's not the same one I grew up in—he sold that one shortly after I moved out. I sometimes wonder if he only kept it for those last few months of my senior year after Mom died because of me. I wasn't such a dick that I didn't notice he was hurting too.

But he'd cheated on her. And that was unforgivable.

I haven't been back to Idaho in a long time, but everything in our small town looks the same. It's only the man who answers the door who looks different. I barely hold back my shock when my dad answers, looking frail, his dark skin ashy and slightly gray, bags under his dark-brown eyes, and his shoulders hunched like it's taking too much energy to answer the door. He looks nothing like the man I remember. His eyes grow damp with tears even as a smile lights his face.

"Dom," he says, with awe and something that sounds strangely like gratitude in his voice. "You came."

"I figured we should do this face-to-face."

He steps back, opening the door wider so I can walk past him. I'm taken aback when I see pictures of me—many that I recognize from the media—plastered on his walls. One from our most recent Super Bowl win, another from when the Fierce Four were featured in a popular sports magazine. My entire career is hung on the wall followed by all my school pictures that my mom used to display. I halt in front of another picture, my heart aching with a deep pain that never seems to go away, but is especially intense when I'm confronted with pictures of my mom.

I remember when this one was taken—only two weeks before my mom was diagnosed with cancer. It was before my whole life started spiraling out of my control. It was after we won the homecoming game, my mom on one side of me, my dad on the other, both of them beaming with pride.

"She loved watching you play."

I startle, ripped from my memories, and turn my head to find my dad staring at the picture with the same kind of pain I recognize every time I think about my mom. It's hard to find my voice over the emotions threatening to choke me.

"I'm surprised you have her picture up."

He turns his sad expression to me, and it's like being hit

by a bulldozer to have the full force of his pain directed at me. "We have a lot to talk about."

He shuffles to the living room and I follow, feeling awkward and uncomfortable. This is not the man I grew up with. That man was larger than life, confident. He walked with a mix of swagger and grace. He always had a smile on his face and a kind word to say. For the first time since I heard his voicemail about his illness, it really hits me that my dad is dying.

He takes a seat on a large, cushioned chair and gestures around the room for me to pick where I want to sit. I choose the beige couch across from him, sitting on the edge, my back stiff and my legs tense. I have to force myself to sit back and attempt to relax in his presence.

"Where's Kim?"

I didn't go to their wedding. I refused on principle. There was no way I could condone him marrying the woman he'd had an affair on my mom with—the woman who'd been my mother's nurse and had become her close friend and confidante. That kind of betrayal didn't deserve to be rewarded, and there was no way in hell I wanted anyone to think I actually supported them. In all honesty, I didn't even think the marriage would last this long.

"She's running some errands."

Good. I'm not eager to see her. I must not hide my disdain well enough because my dad's expression turns sad and disappointed, almost scolding.

"She doesn't deserve your hate. She never did anything wrong."

I scoff. "Yeah, okay. Whatever. Can we just get this over with? What's so important that you needed to harass me for months with calls?"

He leans forward, resting his elbows on his knees,

wincing slightly from an unseen pain at the motion. "I tried for years to find the way to tell you this, but I chickened out and thought I'd have more time. But time is something I'm quickly running out of." He takes a deep breath and on an exhale once again twists the perspective of my world.

"Your mom knew. About Kim," he adds. He leans back in his chair, seemingly trying to find a comfortable position, his cancer clearly already taking a toll on his body. "It was her idea." He shakes his head and looks out the window beside him, but I don't miss the shimmer of tears in his eyes or the way his voice grows hoarse when he speaks. "We'd been together since college. I knew the minute I saw her that she was the woman for me—that I'd marry her and be the happiest man on the planet." He turns back to me, his gaze locking on mine. "And I was. Until she got sick, and I felt completely and utterly helpless. We knew it was terminal, and I think she saw how lost I was starting to feel at just the idea of not having her in my life. I was trying to be strong for her, but your mom..." He stops, a tear escaping down his cheek that he doesn't bother to brush away. I watch his Adam's apple bob as he tries to get his emotions under control. "She knew me better than anyone," he croaks out.

"She fell in love with Kim when we hired her to be her in-home nurse, and she got this harebrained idea that I should date Kim after she was gone. I thought she'd lost her damn mind. The idea of being with anyone else..." He shakes his head. "It was inconceivable. But as the months progressed, she kept pushing for it. Kim and I would find ourselves set up in situations that were orchestrated by your mother. A fancy dinner that she wanted and then claimed she was too tired for, but encouraged Kim and me to enjoy together. A movie night on the couch. A backyard date where we'd lie under the stars. And there was no escaping it because she'd find ways to throw us together. But despite knowing what she was doing, I couldn't quite commit to it. It didn't feel right. Not that I didn't enjoy Kim's company—I did immensely, which made me feel no small amount of guilt.

"But then things took a turn, your mom worsened, and she begged me. *Begged*." He stares out the window again, more tears coming out and his voice hoarse when he finally speaks again. "I was never able to say no to her."

He turns back to me, his heart on his sleeve. "That kiss you saw. It was our first. It wasn't long after she begged me. I learned later she'd been doing the same thing with Kim, who also felt tremendous guilt for starting to fall for her patient's husband. We both had a lot to work through after your mom died, but we couldn't deny that your mom knew what she was doing. We're a good match, and she held me together as I grieved the loss of your mom, as we *both* grieved. She loved your mom, too. We talk about her often.

"I know what you think happened—that I was unfaithful to your mom—but I was only doing what she begged me to do. I never meant for you to see that moment, or for you to know what she was orchestrating. She knew I wouldn't survive without her. I don't doubt for a second that if I hadn't had Kim, I would've wasted away to nothing. I wouldn't have been able to be there for you—not that you needed or wanted me there after what you witnessed. I can't blame you for hating me. It was a complicated and confusing situation for me as well, but I couldn't die without you knowing the truth. I couldn't let you think that my marriage to your mom was anything less than perfect. Because it was." He clears his throat, his brows furrowing with concern. "I'm worried my actions—our actions—have ruined your chance at a healthy and fulfilling relationship." He leans forward again. "That's not what I want for you, son. I want you to find a woman who lights you up the way your mom did for me. I want you to find a woman who knows everything—every good thing you've ever done and every dark skeleton in your closet—and still loves you with every beat of her heart. A woman who knows you better than you sometimes know yourself."

Laney.

I've already found that in a woman, one who's been right in front of my damn face for years.

I lean forward, mirroring his pose, meeting his gaze head-on. "I wish you would've told me sooner, but I've been forced to reflect on my choices lately and can acknowledge I probably wouldn't have heard you out."

"You weren't ready," Dad says with an understanding I'm not sure I deserve.

This whole conversation has gone in a direction I could've never anticipated. I feel his words sink into my bones, my psyche, piercing through all the walls I've built since that day when I witnessed him kiss Kim. All that's left behind as I feel them crumble inside me is a fierce desire to make Laney mine in every way possible. It hits me like a two-ton truck, and an idea—one planted by Emma weeks ago—forms in my mind that might be completely crazy, but sounds better the more I let it take root.

Why waste any more time? I know what I want. I know what Laney's always wanted.

So what if we stopped wasting time? What if she were mine, and I was hers, in every possible way a couple can belong to each other?

I continue my visit with my dad, and we spend the next few hours working to heal years of hurt and making amends.

I end up having dinner with him and Kim before I leave and head to the only other place I've avoided for years.

My mom's gravestone is clean, and a fresh bouquet of flowers sits in a holder next to it. The green grass is freshly cut and there's not another soul around.

I squat down and press my hand to her name. "Hey, Mom," I whisper, emotion hitting me out of nowhere.

"I miss you. I wish you were here so you could see how far I've come. I wish you could see Laney and me together now and how happy we are."

A smile forms on my face. My mom loved Laney. She always said she was the daughter she never had and always wanted. Peace settles over me as I tell her my secret.

"I'm going to ask her to marry me."

THIRTY-THREE

Alayna

It is a truth universally acknowledged that when you get a large group of women together, there's either a lot of laughs, a lot of tears, or both.

Tonight it's tears of laughter as I join the LA Wolves WAGs for our first annual girls' trip to Joshua Tree—because after the first night, Paige insisted this become a yearly tradition. Since none of us are outdoorsy, Paige found us an incredible Airbnb with spectacular views of the desert and plenty of room for all of us.

Nikki brought a karaoke machine with her, which is what's got us all rolling in our seats with tears of laughter at the absolute chaos of us attempting to carry a tune. None of us, except for Emma who's a professional singer, can sing to save our lives, but it's comedic gold watching everyone try.

After my god-awful attempt to sing a popular Taylor Swift song in homage to the Fierce Four—who all think no one but Danae and I know about their love of Swift, when in fact *everyone* knows—I stumble back to the dining room table, more than a little tipsy, and take a long drink of a water.

"Ohmigod, Gina! That dress is gorgeous," Emma exclaims, staring down at Gina's phone.

"Lemme see," I murmur as I move to lean over Emma's shoulder.

It's a picture of Gina standing in front of three long mirrors wearing the most gorgeous wedding dress I've ever seen. She's got the biggest smile on her face and tears in her eyes as she smiles at whoever is holding the camera. Envy hits me first before I push it down and focus on being happy for my friend.

"Gina, you look beautiful," I say.

She beams up at me. "Thanks. I'm so excited to marry him."

"It's about time," Paige says, bumping her shoulder against Gina's. They've been best friends for years, so it's extra cute that they're both with guys on the same team.

"Why has it taken you guys so long to plan the wedding?" Nikki asks, munching on a chip dipped heavily in salsa. Her biggest craving through her pregnancy has been Mexican food. Danae told me Gabe's mom even made her an extra batch of tamales, and she burst into happy tears when they delivered them to her.

"My family," Gina says, rolling her eyes. "They have a lot of opinions about how our wedding should be, and we briefly considered eloping, but honestly, I want the whole big wedding with the giant princess dress. And Will wants it too. So it's just taken a little longer to make sure we're planning the wedding *we* want and not the wedding other people want for us."

Paige looks at Nikki across the table. "When are you and Matt finally tying the knot?"

"After the baby," she says. "I didn't want to be pregnant

in photos. We'll probably get married on the beach sometime next summer."

"And you and Will are getting married this summer?" I confirm with Gina. I can't quite remember the date in my inebriated state.

"Yep, June 13th," she says with a happy sigh.

Pretty soon I'll be the only girlfriend of our WAG group. Although after our Hawaiian vacation, I can't help imagining a wedding of my own. Building a life with Dom, maybe even kids in the future. I grab a chip and dip it in salsa, getting lost in thought and zoning out of the conversation the women around me are having.

"Alayna?"

I glance up and they're all staring at me. "What?"

"Uh-oh," Paige says with a laugh. "She's hit that too-much-to-drink-and-now-she-can't-stay-focused   part   of drunk."

"You either need another drink, or need to switch to water," Emma says, not looking drunk at all, but I know she's had almost as much as I have. God, she's one of *those*—a happy drunk. Whereas, I'm turning into a daydreaming drunk.

I grab the drink in front of Emma and toss it down my throat.

"Hey!" she squeals, but it's too late. I wince and shake my head.

"Oh my God," I choke out. "What the hell was that?"

"A whiskey sour. It's supposed to be sipped and savored not tossed back like that."

"Bleh." I hate whiskey.

"Back to what I was asking," Paige says. "Be honest with us. What's going on with you and Dom?"

There's a hint of genuine concern in her tone that has

me pausing. Does she suspect it started out as fake? There's no way. I thought we managed to hide it pretty well, and then it turned seriously real and there was nothing *to* hide.

"We're together."

She stares at me hard. "I know that. But what I really want to know is how serious is it?" She doesn't have to add the *for him* which hangs unsaid at the end of her sentence. I confessed my real feelings to her once. If anyone could understand falling for your best friend, it's Paige. After all, that's how she and Jack started in high school before he stupidly fucked it up and they were apart for nine years. She also knows how crushing it can be when things don't work out.

Is there really any harm in confessing the whole truth to them? Our relationship isn't a lie anymore which is really the only part that matters.

"It didn't really start out all that great. After the Jen Summers thing, I told Dom I didn't want to be friends anymore, and instead of accepting that, he begged me to fake date him as part of a PR stunt his new rep recommended."

"Hold up," Gina says, raising a hand in a stop gesture. "It's fake? No fucking way. You have to convince that man to give it a real shot."

"It started out fake, but it's not anymore. Honestly, I don't think it ever really was. I've had feelings for him for years, and he's admitted that when I tried to pull the plug on our friendship it made him confront his own buried feelings."

"So where does that leave you two now?" Paige asks, her voice motherly and cautious.

"Now..." I can't stop the smile from growing on my face. "It's the realest thing I've ever experienced." There's a tone of awe in my voice, and all the women around me give me knowing smiles.

They've been in my shoes—maybe not in the exact same situation, but that moment of fear that comes when you take the leap in any serious relationship. The unknown is scary, but it's even scarier when you're putting your entire heart in the hands of someone who could break it. But also that euphoric high that comes with falling in love.

"Although I will admit, a part of me wonders if we're moving too fast," I say as I grab my water bottle because I definitely think it's time to ease off the booze and hydrate.

"What do you mean?" Paige asks.

"It's hard to put into words, but it all just feels really intense and like we've gotten serious quicker than we should've."

"I don't think there's any rule about how fast things should or shouldn't go," Danae says. "Sometimes when it's right, you just know."

I take a sip of my water and stare at the table. My drunk brain plays out some worst-case scenarios and I voice one that's been in my head since my mom planted it there—and despite my best efforts has been harder to dig up than I'd hoped.

"What if he can't be who I need him to be? What if he gets bored with me? He's never had a serious relationship before. Ever."

They're all quiet for a minute before Gina speaks up. "Then we'll be here to support you with whatever you need. But for what it's worth, I think he'll step up for you. These guys can be kind of dense sometimes, but when they finally figure out what they want, they don't give up."

I know she's right. And despite having doubts early on, since the press craziness has died down and we've settled into our real relationship, most of my misgivings have disappeared. I want to believe Dom can be the man I need him to be—the man I've always wanted. I've loved him through his worst years, so why has it been so hard to trust this change? I know he's capable of caring deeply. I remember clearly how he was before his mom died.

Why *did* I doubt him so much? I'm his best friend. I'm supposed to believe in him more than anybody, so what does it say about me that I've been doubting him when he's given me no good reason to?

I get up from the table to grab some of the leftover popcorn before moving to the couch as the next round of karaoke starts.

As if he knows I'm thinking about him, my phone starts vibrating on the side table, his name lighting up on the display.

"I'm gonna take this," I say, picking it up and moving to a quieter part of the house. I answer the call. "Hey, give me a sec."

"Okay."

I go to what's become one of my favorite places in this house, an enclosed patio which right now has a view of the starry night sky that I could never get in LA.

"Okay, found a quiet spot. What's up?"

"Are you having a good time with the girls?" There's a hint of a smile in his voice, and whatever tension I was still carrying in my shoulders evaporates.

"Yeah, I'm having a great time. You saved me from making a further fool of myself by trying to sing."

"Sing?" He actually sounds alarmed, and I fight a chuckle. "Yikes, did you give everyone ear plugs before you started? And why exactly are you singing anyway?"

"Nikki brought a karaoke machine. For some insane

reason, she thought it would be fun, which I suppose it has been but only because we all suck."

"I'm glad you're having a good time."

"I am. Is that why you called? To make sure I was having a good time?"

"Yeah, and I missed you. I wanted to hear your voice."

I melt against the cushioned seat. "I miss you too," I whisper. Then I remember what he had to do today.

"How'd things go with your dad?"

He lets out a sigh and I can imagine him in his hotel room, probably lying on the bed with a hand resting on his hair. "It was surprising."

"Good surprising, or..."

"My mom set him and Kim up. She wanted them together. I didn't really want to believe it, but if you'd seen him, seen the house... He has her picture up. Several in fact. He looked as heartbroken as I feel when he talked about her. And the more I thought about it, the more it made sense. Mom was always looking out for him, taking care of him. She would've hated the idea of him being alone, and I know she loved Kim. Maybe that's why I felt so betrayed when I saw that kiss."

I'll never forget that day, or the effect—both immediately after and long-term—that it had on Dom.

"So what does this mean for you guys now?"

"I don't know." There's silence for a minute before he speaks again. "Do you think it's stupid to take his word for it and forgive him? Is it even possible to put all these years behind us for whatever time he's got left?"

"Well, to your first question, I don't think it's stupid at all. When you're faced with new information, you need to reevaluate your stance and go from there. And to your second question, I think that's ultimately up to you. Can you let it go and let him in?"

"He has newspaper clippings from all my successes framed on his wall." His voice cracks and my heart right along with it. I wish I were there to hold him.

"Dom."

"I want to let him in. I want him to be the dad I grew up believing he was, and I'm worried I've wasted too many years punishing him for something that I didn't understand —that I couldn't have understood." He blows out a breath. "I'm so sick of seeing all the ways I've wasted years of my life. With my dad. With you."

Tears build in my eyes at the misery in his voice—the regret. "We can't go backward, Dom. It's not fair to beat yourself up for the past. All we can do is move forward, and you get to decide how that's gonna go."

"I can't wait to come home to you."

Home.

It's always been wherever he was for me. Even if we lived in separate residences, he's always been my home. Giving him up was always a futile mission.

And I'm so thankful I failed because now our future is brighter than ever.

THIRTY-FOUR

Dominic

"Fuck me, you taste so good," I moan as I slide my tongue along Laney's glistening pussy.

It's official. I'm an addict. And my addiction has only gotten worse since I made the decision to propose. The idea of marrying Laney, being her husband, gets me harder than I ever thought possible.

I've given up on worrying whether that's weird or not. All I know is that since I got back from Idaho, I can't get enough of her.

"Oh my God," she moans as she grips my head, her back arching off the bed and her legs tightening around my ears. "Don't stop. Please don't stop."

Never.

I move my mouth to focus on her plump clit while I slide two fingers inside her. She pulses around me, her orgasm already right on the edge. I curl my fingers to hit that spot I know sets her off, then suck her clit and flick it with my tongue until she detonates with a scream.

I moan into her pussy as I lap up as much of her release

as I can get. I need to get inside her or I'm going to blow in my pants.

I fumble around my side table for a condom while she pants on the bed, recovering from her release, but then I'm sliding inside her and we both groan at the tight feel of being connected.

"Fuck, I love your body. This pussy was made for me."

"Yes," she chants, rocking her hips against mine. I grip her lush ass and tilt it up, so I'm hitting an angle I know sends her through the roof, and sure enough, she sucks in a sharp breath and grips the sheets as a second orgasm rips through her. The feel of her pussy convulsing around my cock is my undoing, and I come with a grunt before collapsing beside her.

After a few moments, Laney breaks the silence. "Is it just me or is sex getting better and better?"

I huff out a laugh. "It's not just you." Then I roll over so I'm on top of her, our pelvises touching but my arms holding most of my weight off her. "Give me five minutes and we can test that theory again."

She smiles wide, and I fall even harder for her. "You're on, Smith."

My phone ringing on my nightstand wakes me up. Without moving my arm from where it rests curled around Laney's naked body, I twist to see who's calling. At the sight of Coach Denton's name, I move swiftly, uncurling from around Laney and trying not to wake her up. I grab my phone and rush out of the room.

"Hello?"

"Smith. It's Denton. I need you to swing by my office today. We need to talk."

My stomach sinks like a rock kicked off a cliff and plummeting to the bottom.

"What time?" I try to keep the nerves out of my voice, but I'm not sure I'm successful. This man and the general manager of the team hold my future in the palms of their hands.

"Sooner the better."

"Got it. I'll get dressed and head over there now." I pull the phone away to glance at the time and wince. Putting the phone back to my ear, I tell him, "It might take me an hour because of morning traffic."

"That's fine. See you soon." He doesn't say goodbye before hanging up on me.

Fuck.

When I walk back into my room, Laney stirs and rolls onto her back, her eyes blinking open slowly before focusing on me as she fully wakes.

"Everything okay?"

I walk to the closet. "Coach Denton just summoned me to his office."

"Oh shit," she says, sitting up and pulling the sheet up to cover her breasts. God, it's tempting to work out my nerves on her gorgeous body and start both our mornings off on the right foot. Especially if I'm about to find out my career with the Wolves is over.

But I'm trying to prove to Denton that I'm reliable, and showing up later than planned because I had sex is definitely not the way to do it.

Instead, I hustle through a shower and getting dressed, then give Laney a quick kiss goodbye before hurrying out to my car.

I'm a wreck the whole drive to the practice facility where Denton has his office. I feel like I'm a dead man walking as my strides eat up the long hallway leading to Denton's open door. He has a second office in the locker rooms at our stadium, but I've always thought this office at our practice facility was way nicer.

I rap on the door with my knuckle, trying to steady my nerves. "Coach?"

"Come on in, Smith."

When I open the door, he gestures to the large chair in front of his desk. I take a seat, not daring to look around the room when I'm trying to prove to him I'm focused and worth keeping.

He leans back in his chair and crosses his arms over his chest. "I've been putting off this conversation."

My stomach drops.

His stern expression doesn't change as he watches my reaction to his words. I try to brace myself for what's coming. I knew this was possible, but it doesn't make it any easier to swallow.

"And I'm glad I did," he continues. "Rich was convinced you were a lost cause."

Rich is our general manager and a real piece of work sometimes.

"But I wanted to give you a little more time to see if you could turn things around. So far, you have. Pretty tremendously I'd say."

He leans forward, and his stern expression feels like it's burrowing into me, trying to suss out anything I might be hiding. "So, I'm going to cut to the point and you better not bullshit me, ya hear?"

I nod.

"Is this for real? Have you really pulled your head out of

your ass or is this just so I won't trade you, and you'll turn back into an idiot once the season gets going?"

I can't even argue with him that I've been an idiot. "This is real, sir."

He arches a brow.

"There's been a lot going on...a lot I haven't handled well, but I'm doing my best to turn things around for good."

"That's what I hoped you would say." He leans back in his chair, and his pose is much more relaxed than it was earlier. "I told Rich if he wants to win another Super Bowl, we need the Fierce Four to remain intact. But Dom, I'll be watching you closely this coming season. Keep up with your workouts and conditioning in the offseason because you have a lot to prove once we get back out on that field."

My shoulders sag as I let out a relieved breath. "Thank you so much, Coach. I won't let you down."

"Better not. I don't like being wrong, especially when it comes to Rich."

"You won't be wrong."

He nods. "Now, tell me what's been going on."

I tell him about my dad—his cancer, not about our strained relationship—and how Laney's ultimatum helped jump-start my conviction to turn things around.

"It's an eye-opener when the one person who's always had your back through any of your fuckups finally has enough. I won't mess up again because I refuse to let her down anymore. I've done that enough."

"I believe you."

Then I do something even more out of character and confide in him. "She's the girl you bring home to meet your parents, the girl you build a life with. I was in no frame of mind for anything that serious before. I wasn't even sure I believed in love."

I don't tell him how witnessing what I thought was my dad's infidelity shaped my beliefs—or lack thereof—about love. But after my talk with my dad, my whole view of relationships has changed. What I grew up believing before I thought he cheated—that true love existed—was real, and now that I'm more convinced than ever I've found my girl, I want to shout it from the rooftops. I can admit I wasn't ready for her—for what we could be—and maybe I never would've been if my life hadn't imploded and I hadn't finally faced my dad and had the tough conversation we needed to have.

Sometimes timing really is everything.

"I can't stop thinking about the future and what I want."

"And what's that?" he asks.

"Her. Plain and simple. To be worthy of her." I glance up at him. "And to be on the Wolves too, of course."

His lips tip up in a grin. "Of course." He leans forward, resting his elbows on his desk. "The love of a good woman can be a powerful motivator. I'm not immune to it, so I get it."

"I'm not going to lose her, and I know if I were to continue to be who I was, I'd lose her completely." I lean forward, mirroring his pose, but with my elbows resting on my spread knees instead of his desk. "I'm done being that guy." There's no doubt in my voice. "I should've been done months ago, but I couldn't seem to get out of my own way."

"I'm happy to hear that, Dom. You're one of my strongest players, and I would hate to lose you." He points a finger. "Now don't let that go to your head."

I chuckle. "I won't, Coach." Sobering, I say, "Thank you. For giving me a second chance. I know I probably don't deserve it, but I'm grateful for it."

"We all make mistakes. As long as you learn from them, then it's not a second chance wasted."

"No, it's not."

This is a second chance I'll never take for granted. We both stand and he comes around his desk and offers me his hand. I shake it, thank him again, and then exit feeling lighter than I have in weeks. Maybe even years.

For the first time in a long time I have a purpose that is more than football. I want to be a man who makes Laney proud, not embarrassed.

Instead of going straight home to Laney, I stop by a jeweler I researched when I got back from Idaho, and after half an hour, I walk out with a ring in my pocket and hope in my heart.

THIRTY-FIVE

Alayna

The door is barely closed before Dom shoves me against it and ravishes my mouth.

"Fuck, I've been dying to kiss you all night," he murmurs as he starts working his way down my jaw to that sensitive spot on my neck that makes my clit hum with pleasure.

"What stopped you?"

We were at another sports dinner tonight, this time for ESPN.

"Too many cameras," he says as he lowers to his knees and pushes my dress up my thighs. "God, I love these thighs." He grips them tight and then buries his head between them, sucking on the lace fabric of my panties. My hands fly to his hair as I tilt my head back, my stomach tightening when that hum turns into a full-on throb.

"This is just for me," he says, his voice deep and husky.

What were we even talking about?

He pulls back, his eyelids heavy with lust. "I'll happily parade you all over the fucking country—hell, the whole damn world—but your lips, every inch of your glorious and perfect body, are just for me."

He keeps his gaze locked on mine as he dips his tongue between my legs, flicking on my pulsing clit. I gasp at the sensation and watch every movement of his tongue, memorizing the image of him looking at me with hunger, possession, and so much love it makes me melt.

He slips a finger inside me as his tongue continues to drive me higher, my legs beginning to shake while I fight off my orgasm.

"Oh God, you're so good at this."

He hums, the sound vibrating against my clit at the same time that he wraps his lips around it and sucks hard. He slides a second finger inside and rotates his wrist so his two fingers are hitting me at a new angle, which combined with him sucking on my clit has me seeing stars as I toss my head back against the door and cry out, coming hard.

He eases me through my orgasm like he always does until it completely ebbs away, and then he sweeps me up in his arms, kissing me while he carries me down the hall to his room. He doesn't break our kiss as he lays me down on his bed, fitting his body between my legs and running his fingers through my hair.

"You have too many clothes on," I mumble, my fingers already moving to the buttons on his white shirt. He nearly had me drooling when he took his suit jacket off earlier and rolled up his sleeves, showing off the thick veins of his forearms.

God, I've always been a sucker for his arms.

He's not the only one who's been holding back all night —I didn't think I'd be able to stop myself if I started kissing him. He's the only man who's ever made me feel both grounded and a little out of control when it comes to how badly I want him all the time. It can't be healthy.

I finish unbuttoning his shirt, and he helps take it off while I move to the button and zipper on his black pants. I pause for a second, eating up the sight of his toned stomach and clearly defined six pack. Unable to stop myself, I lean forward and lick a path up the divot in the middle, loving the way he sucks in a sharp breath and his stomach tenses. My gaze shoots to his, and the desire in his eyes undoubtedly matches my own.

His fingers slide into my hair before he grips it and pulls me back, not enough to hurt, but enough to tell me he's in charge.

He leans down, his lips a breath from mine. "You have no fucking clue what you do to me, do you?"

"Tell me," I whisper, hoping I wreck him even half as bad as he wrecks me—with longing, desire, and a love so intense it leaves me breathless.

His forehead drops to mine, and my heart races even as a calm washes over me. "I'm yours, Laney. All of me, it's yours. I've only ever been and will only ever be yours."

Years. Years I've waited for this moment, and for so long it felt like a waste of time. But right here, right now, with the man of my dreams saying everything I've longed to hear, it feels worth every second of the wait. It's not the first time he's told me this, but every time he says those words, he eases my fears and worries, mainly because those words are just the tip of the iceberg. He's proved it to me with all of his actions since we got together. He's in this one hundred percent.

His lips tilt up in a smile I've only ever seen him give me —a mix of playful, sexy, and sweet. "I'm so in love with you, Laney. You're all I can think about, all I want."

A giddy laugh escapes as I close the distance between us and kiss him with every pent-up ounce of my love. "I love you, Dom," I whisper, my heart feeling immensely full.

Happy tears prick at my eyes. This might be moving fast, but I don't care anymore. I've known him for over a decade, and I've loved him for more than half of that.

Then he swallows thickly, lifts his body up, and drops to one knee in front of me. "I didn't plan to do it like this, but I don't want to wait anymore." He digs in his pocket with one hand while his other reaches for me.

"I've wasted too much time already, and I don't want to waste any more. Laney, I want to build a life with you. I love you more than I ever thought was possible, and while I know I probably don't deserve you, I'll spend the rest of my life trying to be worthy of you." The hand buried in his pocket comes out with a small box that looks vintage, and he flicks it open, showing me the most perfect and gorgeous Victorian-style vintage diamond ring. Tears fill my eyes. Is this really happening?

"Will you marry me?" he asks, his voice strong, love shining in his gaze and making my heart feel so full it could burst.

"Are you sure?"

"More sure than I've ever been about anything in my entire life."

"Yes," I whisper, my throat clogging with more happy tears.

He slides the ring on my finger—a ring that's so perfect you'd think it was made for me—and then surges forward, his lips crashing against mine.

"Move in with me," he mumbles against my lips after he's kissed me thoroughly senseless.

I laugh. "W-what?"

"Move in with me," he says softer, his eyes filled with deep longing. "We spend every night together anyway. You just agreed to marry me. Why wait?"

I pull back slightly so I can get a better look at him. "Are you sure? I know how much you love your space."

"I don't want to be without you, ever."

I smirk. "That sounds a little codependent, Mr. Smith."

He smirks back. "What can I say? I'm addicted to this beautiful blonde who's bewitched me in every possible way."

My smile widens, and I wrap my arms around his neck, loving the feel of my naked breasts against his bare torso. "Who knew you were such a romantic?"

His hands slide down until they squeeze my ass. "You haven't answered my question."

"It didn't sound like a question. It sounded like a demand."

His expression turns earnest. "Will you move in with me?"

I stare into his mesmerizing blue eyes, feeling like I'm living in a dream. Is this really happening? "Yes," I say, barely able to hold back a laugh at how insane this is. Did we really just get engaged and agree to move in together in the span of three minutes?

He surges forward again, closing what little distance there was between us, and kisses me. His tongue slides across the seam of my lips and I part them, my own tongue automatically meeting his as our kiss goes from passionate to salacious. Without breaking the kiss, he pushes his pants down and then grabs a condom he must've had in his pocket and puts it on. He grabs my legs right above my knees and pulls my legs farther apart, making more room for him.

Dom breaks the kiss as he lines himself up at my

entrance and then slides in slowly, his thick cock stretching me wide. Pleasure builds quickly at the perfect way he fills me, and I suck in a breath when he pushes all the way in until he's cradled by my hips.

"Fuck," he murmurs, dropping his forehead to mine, his gaze still locked on where our bodies are joined. "It's never been this good," he says, his voice hoarse. His gaze slides up my body as if memorizing every inch before it lands on mine. "I love you so much."

I stare into his eyes, seeing only truth and complete devotion, and wrap my arms around his neck, pulling him down until our bodies are pressed together. I kiss him sweetly. "Then make love to me, Dom. Show me that I'm yours."

His pupils flare, and he cants his hips back before rocking forward, hitting a spot inside me only he's ever been able to find. My fingernails dig into his back as I meet him thrust for thrust, a glorious pressure building.

"Oh God. I'm gonna come." He moves his lips down the column of my throat, until he gets to that spot near my shoulder that makes me shiver. Goose bumps break out across my arms, my orgasm breaking on a scream. My whole body shakes as he picks up speed, thrusting harder with each pump of his hips until they stutter against me and he holds himself, buried to the hilt. His arms shake as his own orgasm washes over him before he collapses on top of me, kissing me with such reverence it makes my heart soar.

This. This is everything I've ever wanted.

I'm in the bathroom finishing up getting ready for work

when my phone rings on my nightstand. I rush over to grab it but don't recognize the number.

"Hello?"

"Is this Alayna Pritchard?"

"Yes. Who's this?"

"This is Dr. Lakes from Cedars-Sinai. We have your mother here—"

"What?"

"Can you come to the hospital as soon as possible?"

I sit down like a sack of rocks on the edge of the bed. "What's going on?"

"She was dropped off at the ER with low blood pressure, high heart rate, confusion, chills, and difficulty breathing. After running some preliminary tests and observations, we determined she has sepsis and have admitted her."

"She has sepsis? How?"

"It was a result of her recent breast augmentation. It seems she developed an infection that she left too long before seeking treatment."

Leave it to my mom to have a bad boob job that lands her in the hospital with sepsis.

"Wait, you said my mother was dropped off. Does that mean she's there by herself?"

"Yes. We tried to reach out to her boyfriend, who I presume was the man who dropped her off, but he was... uninterested in supporting her at this time. You were the only other emergency contact listed in her phone."

I feel my shoulders sag, and I close my eyes. "I'm on my way," I finally say. The doctor prattles on about the details of where my mom is in the hospital, and I open my eyes to find Dom leaning against the doorframe, his arms crossed, watching me carefully with concern in his eyes.

My heart pangs in my chest. God, I love him so much.

"What's going on?"

"My mom's in the hospital."

When I look back over at him, he's frowning. "Why doesn't she get one of her boyfriends to get her?"

"I don't know. It sounds like Frederic ditched her there. I don't know what's going on, but the hospital made it sound serious."

"Do you want me to come with you?"

I love him even more for offering, but I need to handle this myself. She's my problem, even if I wiped my hands of her. I'll help her get a plan in place for when she gets discharged and then we'll go back to our nonexistent relationship.

"No, that's okay." I give him a quick kiss. "I'll text you with updates, but hopefully this won't take too long."

When I finally get to the hospital, I learn that things with my mom are not nearly as simple as the doctor made it sound on the phone.

"She's developed a secondary infection. We're treating it, but she's not responding well to the meds," the doctor says as I stare at my mom sleeping in her bed. There are dark circles under her eyes, but for the first time in a long time, she looks like the mother I grew up with before my dad died and our lives changed drastically.

"What does that mean?" I ask, forcing my gaze away from my mom and to the doctor standing patiently on the other side of her bed.

The doctor looks at me with sympathy. "It means things are up in the air right now unless she responds to the meds the way we need her to."

"So, um," I flounder, unsure what to say, and rub my forehead. "I don't know what to do," I confess.

"There's not much to do but wait at this point."

"Right."

"Is there anyone else to call?"

I look over at my mom. Our relationship might be complicated, but for a woman who's prided herself on never being alone, there's something especially heartbreaking knowing I was the only one who would come to her side.

"No, there's no one else."

The doctor nods and then steps out, leaving me to the quiet beeping of my mom's heart monitor. I pull the chair in the corner of the room up to her bed and sit, holding her hand, which is unusually cold.

Or is it? I guess I wouldn't know. I can't remember the last time I held her hand.

The room is bare and sterile, exactly what you'd expect from a hospital room, and something about it feels especially depressing. As the day drags on and my mom's condition worsens instead of improves, my emotions start to get the better of me. My mom and I may have had a complicated relationship, but I never imagined I'd be in this kind of position.

I don't want to be here alone. I should've taken Dom up on his offer.

I pull my hand from my mom's and reach for my phone in my purse. It takes me longer than it should to pull up Dom's contact and finally press the button because my hands are suddenly shaking, and my chest heaves with barely restrained sobs. It's like that day at the restaurant when my mom walked away from me but a million times worse, and I don't really understand why I'm losing it like this.

It only rings once before he says, "Laney?"

The smooth cadence of his voice is an instant balm to the fear that is wreaking havoc through my system.

"I need you," I say, my voice hoarse and barely audible.

He's immediately on alert. "Where are you?"

I tell him and then hang up because I can't stop shaking or speak through the tears streaming down my face. My fingers are suddenly freezing cold—in fact, the whole room feels cold and achingly lonely. I bury my head in my hands and rock back and forth in the uncomfortable chair for I don't know how long before strong arms wrap around me.

I look up into Dom's bright blue eyes, his jaw clenched like granite, as he lifts me up, holding me tight against his body before settling in the chair with me in his lap, just like he did the last time I saw my mom. His arms tighten around me, and I'm infused with his warmth. I wiggle my arms from where they're trapped against his chest and wrap them around his neck, holding him as close to me as I possibly can.

"Thank you for coming."

"There's nowhere else in the world I want to be but wherever you are."

THIRTY-SIX

Dominic

We're sitting with our bodies parallel on the sturdy cot the nurse rolled in for us, Laney tucked into my side with her head resting on my shoulder. They were going to force her out, but being semi-famous has its perks, and I was finally able to use all the media attention on me for something good. Laney's mom still rests in her bed, the heart monitor and the stuttered rise and fall of her chest the only signs she's still alive. She hasn't woken in the twenty-four hours that we've been here, and unfortunately her condition hasn't gotten better, so it's been a lot of waiting for what seems like more bad news every time the doctor comes in here.

The TV is on, playing quietly in the background on an entertainment news channel since there's nothing else on. I've got my eyes closed when Laney stiffens against me. I open them at the same time she grabs the remote to turn up the volume, her eyes glued to the screen.

"It looks like there's another Hollywood baby on the way. Jen Summers just announced she's pregnant, but the real question is: Who's the father? Not long ago, she was caught

having an affair with none other than LA Wolves cornerback Dominic Smith."

"It was quite the scandal, Steve. If you recall, her husband caught them in the act."

My teeth grind together as the two entertainment news anchors—are they even called news anchors if they only sling rumors and gossip about what's going on in Hollywood?—speculate about whether I'm the father of Jen Summers's baby.

Laney pulls away from me, standing up and walking toward the door before I can even reach out to grab her.

"I'm getting some water," she mumbles right before she swings the door open and disappears into the hall.

I run my hands over my face before pushing myself up to standing and chasing after her. "Fuck this," I mutter, annoyed and irritated Jen is letting this bullshit go out to the media after I made sure her name wasn't slandered further while I tried to fix my reputation.

Her baby is not mine, and she knows it.

"Laney, wait," I call out, right as she rounds the corner into a small room that has a couple of vending machines and a few chairs for those looking for quiet.

She doesn't even spare me a glance. "What is it?" She's trying to act unaffected—not well, but trying nonetheless—but the resignation in her voice still guts me.

I grab her arm just above her elbow and spin her to face me. "It's not mine."

She shrugs, not meeting my gaze. "It's none of my business."

"Bullshit."

That gets her gaze. Her eyes are filled with fury and hurt, and all I want is for her to unleash it all on me. I deserve it after years of never seeing her the way she deserved to be seen.

"Let it out, Laney. Tell me how you really feel," I prod.

She puts her hands on my chest and shoves me back, before pushing those delicate fingers that have traced every inch of my skin into her hair, her eyes everywhere but on me. She paces back and forth for a second before facing me and letting me have it.

Fucking finally.

"I hate this. I hate that you stuck your dick in every supermodel in LA. I hate that I know about all the women you've been with and that never once did you look at me like that until I tried to end our friendship. I hate that some-times I wonder if this is going to last because you've never been serious about anyone before. And I *hate* that you were with Jen Summers and now she might be having your baby when the only woman who should be having your baby is me. I hate it, Dom."

I swallow thickly, feeling each of her words like a strike to the heart. "I get it. I hate all of that too. But that baby isn't mine."

She rolls her eyes. "You can't say that definitively."

"Actually, I can. We'd have had to have sex to make a baby."

She opens her mouth to argue, but then snaps it shut, staring at me in shock. "Y-you never...?"

I shake my head. "Her husband did catch me with my pants literally down around my ankles because I had just started undressing. Nothing had happened except for a heavy make-out session." I grip the back of my neck, debating whether to tell her the rest. At this point, the only thing I have to lose is Laney, which isn't an option.

"I'm embarrassed to admit I struggled to get hard.

Maybe it was the booze, maybe not, but I couldn't keep it up, so we just made out and then we were going to try being naked when I already knew I should've called it quits. And that just happened to be the moment her husband got home, something I suspect she knew was coming based on the look on her face."

She stares at me, and I hold her gaze so she can see the truth in my eyes. Her shoulders sag, most of her fury dissipating but the hurt still remaining.

"But it's not just the women, is it?" I ask.

"You didn't appreciate me. For years, you took advantage of how much I did for you, never really acknowledging it."

I step closer to her, desperate to touch her, to ground myself. "You're right. I didn't. I took you for granted in every way possible, and I'll have to live with that for the rest of my life. Knowing all the time I wasted not loving you as fiercely as you deserved. Not treating you like the gift you are."

Another step. This time, close enough that our toes touch. She looks up at me, tears welling in her eyes.

"But I'm going to love you with every breath I take for the rest of my life. I know I don't deserve you, Laney, but you're all I want, and that's never going to change."

"How do you know?" she whispers as a tear slips free. I reach up and brush it away with my thumb.

"Because you are the only woman I've ever wanted to come home to. The only one I've ever called at the end of a long day. The only one I've ever confided in. You are my heart and soul. Without you, I'm nothing. I might've been dumb not to see you for what you always were before, but you've got to admit, I'm not a guy who typically makes the same mistake twice." I drop my forehead to hers. "When it comes to your heart, I will never do anything to risk losing that. Please, Laney. Have a little faith in me. I promise I won't let you down. Not again."

"I'm scared, Dom. I'm scared I'm not going to be enough for you."

I pull back, my brows furrowed. "Where the hell would you get the idea that you aren't enough for me?" Her gaze drops, but not before she glances toward the door leading back to her mom's room. My jaw clenches. I knew she was messing with Laney's head, but to make her daughter feel like she's not good enough for me is bullshit.

Fuck that.

I lift my hand, tucking it under her chin until her eyes finally meet mine. Fuck, I want to get lost in those deep pools of blue for the rest of my life.

"It's not you who needs to prove you're enough. You're more than enough. You're so out of my league, it's not even funny. Don't ever doubt that, Sunshine. You're my light. Screw what anyone else says," I say, pointedly glancing toward her mom's room before looking back at her. "I'm yours, until my last breath and final heartbeat."

Her shoulders sag, but not in defeat this time—in relief. I wrap my arms around her shoulders, pulling her tight to my body. She wraps her arms around my waist, and every-thing feels right in the world. For so long, I convinced myself I needed football to be worthy or have purpose.

I was so wrong.

All I've ever needed is her.

THIRTY-SEVEN

Alayna

We end up needing Shawna's help when the press learns where Dom is and storms the hospital. Everyone wants a sound bite from him about Jen Summers's pregnancy announcement.

It takes everything in me to bite my tongue instead of lashing out. My mom's condition is deteriorating every hour, and every time I hear Jen Summers's name, I want to scream.

To his credit, Dom does everything to shield me from the drama without ever leaving my side. At some point, he gets extra security to come to the hospital to ensure that nobody even gets to our floor. The TV remains off, and the staff are professional enough not to bring it up.

Which I'm grateful for, especially when the moment we've all been dreading arrives. Mom passes the point of no return, her condition suddenly deteriorating until she takes her last breath. I stare at her chest, willing it to move. We may not have had a good or healthy relationship, but I didn't want her to die.

The nurses quietly turn off the machines. "Take all the

time you need," one says to Dom as my gaze remains locked on the unmoving body of my mother.

Dom wraps his arms around me, and I hadn't even noticed how cold I'd gotten until I feel his warmth. That's what sets off the tears again.

My body sags, but he's there to catch me, lifting me up and holding me in his arms as I completely fall apart.

"Let it all out. I've got you, Laney."

I know he does, which makes me feel even more foolish for my outburst when I first found out about Jen's pregnancy. He's always had me, but his actions prove it even more than his words.

He's changed, and I need to stop throwing his past sins in his face when I get scared, because that's really what my reaction was about. I was scared that we'd be stuck with Jen Summers in our life forever. That she'd always have a piece of him that I wanted all for myself.

I let myself cry for a few more minutes before I pull myself together, but even as the tears dry up, I remain curled up in Dom's arms. My happy place.

"I'm sorry about earlier."

"You have nothing to apologize for," he says softly before dropping a tender kiss to my hair.

I pull away enough to look in his gorgeous eyes. "Yes, I do. You did nothing to deserve me lashing out at you just because Jen Summers likes drama. I don't want your past to always be hanging over our heads. I forgive you, Dom. I forgive you for treating me poorly when your head was so far up your ass you couldn't see the light of day."

He laughs and I can't help smiling at the reaction I was hoping for. "From this day forward, we start with a clean slate. The Dom and Laney of our past will always be there, but their decisions and fears no longer define us or our relationship, okay?" I ask.

It's exhausting to hold on to all those feelings of frustration and anger about how things played out in the past. Just like I didn't want my mom's words to poison my thoughts, I don't want our past actions to poison our future success as a couple.

Because I have no doubt we'll be the strongest couple I know if we allow ourselves to be.

He smiles at me—his soft smile that makes me feel all mushy inside. "It's a deal."

My mother's funeral is sad because not a single one of her supposed "friends" shows up, even after I called everyone listed in her phone, hoping to find someone who knew her and would come.

Instead, as we stand in the cool spring air, Dom on one side and Tessa on my other, we're surrounded by my LA Wolves family. Even though today is supposed to be about her, I can't help feeling the endless love of my friends who are gathered around to support *me* even when most of them never met my mom. Today only further cements that they're more than friends—they're my family, and like I learned a long time ago, sometimes your found family is stronger than any blood family ever could be.

I place a white lily on her casket, then the pastor says his final words and the whole thing is over. It took less than twenty minutes to close another chapter of my life, but as Dom holds my hand on the way back to the car, I feel a lightness encompass me, and I hope wherever my mom is, she feels lighter too. I hope she's with my dad, finally happy.

After the service, we all go back to Dom's house where he's had a whole catered spread delivered. For so long, I was convinced I had to do everything myself and support myself, but I can't deny it's nice being able to let someone else take the reins sometimes. The way Dom has seen to all my needs this past week has made me love him even more, which I didn't think was possible.

We spend the next several hours eating, talking, even laughing, and despite the heaviness for why we were all gathered together in the first place, the day ends on a high note.

Especially when I end the night, curled up in bed with Dom, right where I've always belonged.

"You ready for this?" Mr. Smith asks me as he holds out his hand.

I smile wide, my heart full to bursting. "So ready."

I put my hand in his, and he pats it with his other hand before wrapping my arm around his elbow and walking with me toward our destination.

We round the corner, and I suck in a sharp breath. Dom stands at the end of the sand aisle, wearing tan pants and a white button-down that he's rolled up his forearms as I requested because I love that look on him.

I love any look on him.

I love him. Plain and simple as that.

His jaw clenches and emotion fills his eyes as they brim with tears. There's so much love shining through his gaze that remains locked on me as I make my way down the aisle, his dad walking next to me.

He and Dom have been working hard on their relationship since the revelation about how Dom's mom influenced Kim and his dad getting together. And since we wanted to share this important memory with him before his cancer got worse, we decided not to wait any longer to get married.

I was touched when Mr. Smith offered to escort me down the aisle and give me away. It had always broken my heart to think about walking down the aisle by myself—a feeling of loneliness that only got worse after my mom died —and he took away that burden. He holds me steady as we walk closer to his son, my own tears blurring my vision.

I blink them away so I can clearly see the man I'm walking toward. The man I've always walked toward.

He shifts back and forth before taking two steps to meet me and close the gap.

I laugh. "You were supposed to wait for me to get to you."

"I couldn't wait anymore."

He slides a hand around my waist, pulling me closer to him, then smiles at his dad. "Thank you," he says, his voice teary, but happy.

"Anything for you, son," he says, his own voice choking up as father and son share a brief silent moment.

We've come a long way in the past few months.

Dom gazes down at me, brushing away a stray tear and then holding my cheek like I'm the most precious thing in the world to him. "You look beautiful, Sunshine."

"I love you," I whisper. I never thought I'd be so emotional, but I'm struggling to keep it together.

Dom smiles down at me. "Let's do this. It's about damn time I became your husband."

"Hear, hear!"

I laugh and glance over at Tessa, the one whose shout only added to the perfection of this day. When I told her our secret plan to elope, she was on board and helped me get everything coordinated.

We decided to steal a play out of Luke and Emma's playbook and caught a plane to Hawaii. Only Tessa, Dom's dad, and his dad's wife, Kim, are here to support us today. And that's just the way we wanted it.

No press. No fanfare. Just us and a few witnesses.

We'll hold a reception later—probably after the season since Dom's got to get to training camp next week, immediately after our honeymoon.

"Are you two ready?" the officiant asks us.

Dom and I make eye contact, both of us smiling. "Definitely," we say at the same time, eliciting a laugh from everyone around us. We step closer to the officiant who's standing under an arch covered in beautiful dark-pink hibiscus flowers. The ocean is at his back, the sun hanging low but not setting yet.

He goes through the usual ceremony pieces, but then he gets to the vows, which we've opted to do our own.

"Alayna, you go first."

I release my hands from Dom's—who's been holding me tight like he's afraid I'll dash out of here without him—and turn to Tessa who hands me the piece of paper with my vows typed neatly.

I swallow the emotion already building up as I bare my heart and soul to this man.

Grabbing his ring from Tessa, I slide it on his left ring finger as I begin to speak. "Dom, you are my rock. My heart. But I have a confession. I thought you were a dumb jock before we started that group project junior year." Everyone laughs, and Dom smiles and shakes his head at me. "And then I got to know you. It's really no surprise I fell in love with you. Your heart is as big as your love for football. You dedicate yourself to those you care about, and when you make your mind up about something, there's not a single person in the world who could stop you. We've had our ups and downs—some higher and lower than others—but at the end of the day, you're my person. You're the only man I want by my side for the rest of my life. I love you, Dom."

He steps forward, cupping my face in his hands, and kisses me fiercely. The officiant clears his throat, but Dom doesn't pull back until he's good and ready. When he finally breaks the kiss, he drops his forehead to mine.

"My turn. I *was* a dumb jock." He pulls away enough to stare into my eyes, his expression apologetic but determined, and still that love shining endlessly. "Because I didn't see you for what you always were to me until it was almost too late. I promise to never take you for granted. To love you with everything I am. I promise to stand by your side, chasing any dream you want. To build a life with you that surpasses anything you've ever imagined. I can't promise that I won't ever mess up, but I can promise to always learn from my mistakes. And I promise that no one will ever love you as much as I do because you are my whole world, Laney. I know you think football is at the top, but it's not. You are. You always have been. Nothing means anything without you, and I will spend the rest of my life proving my love to you."

Tears stream down my face—there's no use stopping them. He pulls my wedding band from his pocket and slides it on my finger to join my engagement ring, which I refused to take off, and then leans forward again, resting his forehead on mine and staring into my eyes. "I promise to always see you for the gift that you are. I'm yours. Always. Forever."

When there's nothing but the sound of the waves

crashing on the beach, the officiant clears his throat again and we pull apart enough to give him our attention. He smiles wide.

"I now pronounce you husband and wife. You may kiss the bride."

Dom doesn't need any further prompting. He closes the short distance between us and kisses me with all the passion and love in the world. Everything fades as I fall into his kiss, the most perfect kiss I've ever experienced.

He pulls back, a wide grin lighting up his face, and I finally notice that everyone is clapping and cheering for us.

It's the perfect day.

A perfect wedding with a man who's imperfect, but perfect for me.

And it's already better than anything I ever imagined.

Some people speculate about our whirlwind romance, especially the tabloids, but I know the truth. It's the same reason I never gave up on him. The reason he never seriously dated anyone else. The reason we always chose each other at the end of each day.

Dom and I were always destined to be together. We were as inevitable as the chaos on the football field after the snap.

Alayna

I'm bending over to check on the lasagna I've got cooking in the kitchen when I hear a grumble behind me and then two strong hands grip my hips, pulling me back against his pelvis where I can feel the stiffness of his erection. I shut the door of the oven with a laugh and straighten up.

Dom pulls me snug against his body and murmurs against my ear, "Do you have any idea how sexy you are?"

"I'm sure you're going to tell me," I say with a smile in my voice.

He kisses behind my ear and then my neck. "The sexiest woman alive."

"Well, then I guess we're a perfect match since you just got nominated as one of People's Sexiest Men Alive."

He spins me around and kisses me deeply. My arms wrap around his neck as I melt into his kiss. Fifteen years married and this man still makes me weak in the knees.

"Oh, gross! Can't you two give us some warning when you're going to make-out in the kitchen? Seriously!"

We break away with a chuckle as Dom spins us to face

our eleven-year-old son, Ryder. His twin brother stands next to him looking at us with such disappointment, I can barely keep my face straight.

Ryder and Zeke are spitting images of their dad, and despite both of them having completely different personalities, in this, they are united. Both standing with their arms crossed as they scold us in that way only eleven-year-olds can because they caught us—again.

"Ry!" Our eight-year-old daughter cries and Ry's tough exterior immediately fades as he attends to his little sister, Talia.

I lean against my husband, my heart so full, as I watch Ry and Zeke soothe their sister as she shares her distress about missing her favorite doll. With one more look of disappointment at us—which has me turning my head into Dom's chest to muffle my laughter—the boys take their sister to go hunt for her missing doll.

"I swear, I love these kids more than anything else, but goddamn they're such little cockblocks sometimes."

There's no way to muffle the snort that escapes, and then we're both giggling.

"Come on," he says, grabbing my hand and sneaking us through the back hallway and up the stairs toward our room.

"Dom! We can't," I hiss, worried the kids will see us and give us even more grief.

He spins around with a wicked smile. "They're helping Tali and you know she's going to make them play with her, and they'll go along with it because, let's face it, our daughter has her brothers wrapped around her little finger."

"God, she really does." I feel for the poor guy who falls in love with her.

"So, we have roughly twenty minutes before one of

them comes hunting for us." His wicked smile grows wider. "I can make you come at least twice in that time."

"Those are some big promises."

"Is that a challenge, Mrs. Smith?"

My heart flutters the way it always does when he calls me that. Fifteen years later and I still get giddy hearing it.

"You bet your ass it is, Ace."

He laughs and then throws me over his shoulder as if I weigh nothing—which couldn't be farther from the truth after the hell having three kids put my body through—and jogs the rest of the way to our room. I giggle as his shoulder shakes from his own laughter. Then we burst into our room and he sets me down at the edge of our bed, both of us breathless from laughing.

His eyes heat and flare as he stares down at me, his thumb brushing across my bottom lip. "I love you so much, Laney."

I tilt my head into his palm where he holds me tenderly as we stare at each other. I didn't think it was possible to love him any more than I did when we first got together, but in our years together our love has only grown.

That's not to say our marriage has always been sunshine and roses. It hasn't.

But every day—even the hard ones—we choose each other. We made vows to each other that we've spent every day of the last fifteen years making sure we honor. And through the highest highs and lowest lows, our love has grown, the roots strengthening with each obstacle we faced and overcame together.

And there's no one on earth I'd rather fight with and love than this man right here.

"Kiss me, Mr. Smith," I murmur, already leaning toward his lips. He meets me in the middle and then any other words we could speak disappear as we let our bodies do the talking.

He pushes me back on the bed, slipping off my yoga pants and underwear in the process, and then his mouth is licking up the seam of my pussy and my head tips back at the pleasure that builds. It's slower than it used to be—thanks to aging—but he never gives up on making me come with his mouth before he buries himself inside me.

A gasp escapes when he plunges two fingers in at the same time that he sucks my clit and that pressure in my core grows.

"Oh God, Dom," I shudder as he does this swirl-flick thing with his tongue, his fingers thrusting in and out relentlessly all the while rubbing against the fleshy spot inside that never fails to send me tipping over the edge.

I grip his head to my body as my orgasm washes over me, leaving me a panting mess on the bed.

He kisses up my body, pushing my shirt up over my bra, and then tugging down the cups so he can suck on my nipples.

He groans. "God, Sunshine, your body makes me feel feral. I can't get enough." He sucks my nipple hard until it pops out of his mouth, his eyes dazed with lust and then his lips are on mine while his hands fumble with his belt.

I used to be self-conscious about my breasts because they were never the same after the twins, but Dom always makes it clear he appreciates the way my body changed after kids.

It's just another thing that makes me love him more with every day that passes. I swear, only Dominic Smith could drive me crazy and make me love him more all in the same day. But I wouldn't have it any other way.

He shoves his pants down and then brushes his fingers over my sex to make sure I'm ready for him before he positions his thick cock at my entrance and then in one smooth thrust he buries himself to the hilt. We both moan at the exquisite feel.

"Dom," I moan, my pelvis tipping up trying to encourage him to move.

"Christ, Laney. Your pussy is perfect."

He finally moves—thank God—and starts with a slow rhythmic pace. Then we hear the kids shout and both of us freeze for a split second before we make eye contact and then he's frantically thrusting in and out.

"Damn kids aren't going to ruin this. You better come on my cock, and you better come fast."

He slides a hand between us to rub on my clit as he starts to aggressively pound into me. With him touching my clit, it takes no time at all for my second orgasm to crash through me. With one more thrust, he comes hard, groaning into my neck.

His body shudders as he weakly holds himself over me. "Fuck. I wish I could stay buried in you all day."

I tap his chest with some urgency. "Me too, but I'm guessing we have less than a minute before the kids come looking for us, so we need to get dressed quick."

He drops one more brief kiss to my lips and then pulls away with a smile. We both frantically try to clean up and get our clothes back to rights.

"You good?" He asks, his hand on the handle of our bedroom door.

I nod.

He opens the door and we both freeze as three kids stand outside the door. Talia holds her doll staring innocently—and slightly confused—between her brothers and us. Her brothers, on the other hand, look less than impressed.

"I told you they were probably in their room," Zeke says. "Let me guess. You lost something again?"

"And only dad could help you find it," Ryder adds.

They had the puberty and sex talk at school this year and ever since they give us dirty looks whenever they think we've been doing something naughty.

To be fair, catching us after we've just had sex doesn't happen often, but these two sure do like to give us grief when it does.

"I had to talk to Mom about your Christmas presents and I didn't want you two nosey Nelly's to hear."

I nibble the inside of my lip, but know better than to say anything. I'm a terrible liar and these boys can read me better than any book.

But it's clear they don't entirely believe their dad's lie either.

"Sure, ya were. Whatever. Adults are gross." Ryder shivers in disgust.

Zeke nods in agreement. "Can we play outside?"

Dom nods and the three kids turn and run down the stairs. We hear the back door open and then close behind them.

"They're totally on to us," he says, looking down at me.

"Yup."

He wraps his arm around my waist, pulling me flush against his body. "I hope someday they find a partner they can't keep their hands off of, and then I'll give them a bunch of shit about it."

"Real mature, Dom."

"What's the fun of having kids if you can't turn the tables on them when they're older."

I roll my eyes and shake my head while a little laugh escapes.

Then I curl into my husband's arms, wrapping mine around his waist and soaking in his warm.

There's not a thing I'd change about our life.

Our happily ever after.

AFTERWORD

Funny story. I once thought I was in love with my best guy friend in college.

I wasn't.

He was "safe" and someone I trusted with my life. And honestly, I can look back and see we would've been an absolutely god awful couple. But I was a mess and, at the time, safe looked pretty good. Unfortunately "safe" came with a lot of confusion and heartache. Writing this book took me back to all those messy feelings I had back when I was in college.

I thought writing Dom and Laney's story would be hard because I knew I would be pulling from that part of my past for inspiration, but it wasn't. I loved writing Dom and Laney's story and redeeming the player. I loved how once Dom pulled his head out of his ass, he was all in.

I'm a big believer that people's actions speak louder than their words, and I wanted to convey that for these two. I wanted Dom to prove to Laney that he loved her with his entire being, not with pretty words, but with bold and deliberate actions.

I hope I succeeded in that.

I also need to do a quick thank you to all the people who made this book possible.

First and foremost, my husband, my happy ever after. Through the highest highs and lowest lows, I will always choose you.

To my miracle babies L & A, who inspire me to be my best self for them every day.

To my editors, Ann Suhs and Ann Riza, for always making my books the best possible versions they can be.

To my amazing cover designer, Kate Farlow for designing the series covers and kicking ass at it.

To my beta readers and ARC team for your support and feedback.

And to you, my reader, for joining me on this crazy journey and loving my books. I'm infinitely thankful for you!

LA WOLVES FOOTBALL

In the Grasp

Across the Middle

Down by Contact

Taking the Handoff

LA WOLVES DEFENSE

Scorched Turf (author website exclusive novella)

Defending the Backfield

After the Snap

Closing the Distance

Protecting the Boundary

RAPTUROUS INTENT ROCKSTARS

Noble Intent

Forbidden Intent

Devoted Intent

Promised Intent

BREAKING THE RULES

Only a Kiss

Just for Tonight

About Last Night

CFU HOCKEY

Campus Crush

Campus Rival

MEADOWBROOK, MT

One Weekend in Montana